The Girlz of $\mathcal{G}$alstanberry

By

Garen S. Wolff

To: Dorilyn
From: G. Wolff
10/13/10
Enjoy!

WolffHouseBooks & Publishing
www.GalstanberryGirlz.com
Copyright © 2010 by Garen S. Wolff
Illustrations by Thornpallette copyright © 2010 by
Garen S. Wolff
Editor: Alyssa A. Bell
Book layout: John A. Koziatek

ISBN-13: 978-0-615-39129-8
ISBN-10: 061539129X

Printed in the U.S.A.
First edition, September 2010

Dedication

This book is dedicated to my outstanding parents,
Dr. Mervin Wolff and Mrs. JoAnne S. Wolff.
Without their love, encouragement and financial support,
this book would not be possible!

Many thanks to my relatives, with special gratitude
to my aunt, Cheryl Slay, Esq. for her legal expertise
and guidance.

And last, but not least, to my City Preppies and girls
from around the world, that inspire me everyday
to tell their story (& my story as a tween!).

Galstanberry Girls Academy Motto

*"May all Galstanberry Girls pursue their dreams,
stand their ground, persevere through obstacles,
and live without regret"*

Contents

Gal-stan-ber-ry (gawl-stän-ber-ee) n. 1. a person
that possesses strong intellect, wit and leadership skills.
—adj. 2. sweet, bold, unique [2010, Ameri.]

The Berry Beginning...

Monday, June 31, 1926

"**I**s she okay? I hear no sound! NO SOUND!" Mr. Galstanberry shouted as he wrung his hands and feverishly paced back and forth across the Tabriz carpet, a recent $200,000 purchase from the renowned auction house, Sotheby's. Although that was close to a million in 1926, it was mere pennies to the vast Galstanberry fortune. However, money wasn't the only inheritance. Charles Galstanberry was a statuesque 6'3, with emerald eyes, and chestnut hair that had just a hint of curl.

The Galstanberry twenty-acre estate rose up from the horizon like a French château with interconnected balustrades and high-spiraling turrets that seemed to touch the clouds. It was flanked by a magnificent rose garden and horse stables.

Dr. Wilshire emerged from the master suite and wiped his brow with a golden handkerchief. "She's fine, despite her weak immune system. But babies, well sir, they take time."

"Whatever it takes, doctor! I want a healthy boy!" Suddenly, a loud scream emitted from the Victorian double doors.

"Dr. Wilshire! Dr. Wilshire! I think it's time!" The nurse yelled with great urgency. The doctor slapped the expecting father's back, "When I return, you shall have a son!"

Mr. Galstanberry puffed out his chest and admired a self-portrait that hung above the fireplace in the library.

What will I teach Andrew first? How to play polo?
Or perhaps how to shoot a deer?

To his right, a staircase spiraled up to bookcases and down to his prolific hunting collection in the cellar. Andrew's life had been entirely mapped out. All he needed to do was overcome the very first obstacle—his mother's birth canal. After what seemed like an eternity, Mr. Galstanberry yelled, "What's going on in there?" The baby cried as if cued.

That's my boy!

He delicately buttoned his suit coat and closed a fourteen-karat gold pocket watch. Dr. Wilshire rubbed his forehead as he re-entered the library. "The child, uh, is with your wife."

"My God, Henry! What took so long? What's wrong?!" But before the doctor could respond, he rushed into the suite. Mrs. Galstanberry looked up with tears lingering in her bright blue eyes. "We have a girl, Charles! And she is absolutely beautiful!"

"Girl?" He repeated in disbelief. Immediately, the room began to spin. His head felt heavy, throat became dry and legs buckled from the overwhelming wave of disappointment.

Ten minutes later, he blinked his eyes to distinguish a blurry Dr. Wilshire and nurse hovering above him. "He's regaining consciousness!" Mrs. Galstanberry sighed annoyingly. "Charles, what on Earth is wrong with you?! I'm the one who just gave birth! Me, your wife, re-mem-ber?!" He blushed with embarrassment and brushed the dust from his suit. "Sorry, dear, where is my Andrew?" His arms shot out to hold the infant. Instead, the doctor led him to a chair. "Sir, I have some cold water with a fresh le—"

"Do not distract me! I want my SON!"

Mrs. Galstanberry chuckled. "Andrew?! No, Charles, dear, meet Aun-drea!" She flashed a giant smile and handed over his daughter.

"Aun-drea? Aun—Doctor, let me talk to my wife in private." When Dr. Wilshire left, Mr. Galstanberry sat and wept quietly while rocking the infant. "Charles, you are terribly embarrassing! I am alive and our child is perfectly healthy." She closed the clasp to her pearl necklace and reached for the matching bracelet—labor would not put a damper on her style. "I know, dear, but—"

"But nothing! With my health problems, it's a miracle that we even have a child! It's a girl, just get over it!" He shook his head in confusion. "Eleanor, who will inherit my company?" She removed the jeweled handheld mirror from the glass bed stand and fixed her blonde tresses. "Aundrea, of course!"

"Who will I teach polo? That is a man's sport, you know." She took a sip of cranberry juice, and then sighed, "Aundrea will be the best polo player Connecticut has ever seen!" It seemed like she had an answer to everything.

"Well, Yale does not educate women and any child of mine deserves the best. Even if it's a girl, I suppose." He looked down at his polished opal loafers.

"You suppose?! Charles Jefferson Galstanberry, a woman doesn't have to settle for governess anymore, she can be a professor! Or, be a doctor instead of a midwife!" She stopped admiring her nails and looked at him with great seriousness.

"Aundrea will have the best, won't she?"

"Of course, dear, I—"

"And you will ensure that she follows her dreams, right, dear?"

"Indeed, Eleanor, I—"

"It's settled then, every tutor will be at her complete disposal." She returned the mirror to the bed stand and placed the back of her hand flat against her forehead.

Dr. Wilshire reappeared with a fresh glass of water and a lemon slice. "How are you feeling?" He removed the infant from Mr. Galstanberry's arms. "It's a lot to take in but—"

"No, Mr. Galstanberry, I was asking your wife."

"Oh, of course, of course!" He bit into the lemon and puckered his lips.

"Doctor, I am quite cold and my limbs feel limp."

"Well, it's normal for you to feel tired."

Dr. Wilshire rubbed his chin and placed a hand on her forehead. "But, that's a fever alright! Remain in bed until I return next Sunday. Instruct your kitchen staff to prepare fresh fruits and vegetables for every meal. Also, drink as much warm milk as you can. Tomorrow, my nurse will bring by some aspirin. Take two daily with water—one in the morning, and one in the evening."

Mr. Galstanberry's fountain pen rapidly wrote the doctor's instructions on parchment paper. "Charles, your wife will need your undivided attention." Mr. Galstanberry nodded earnestly in response.

• • •

As the week progressed, Mr. Galstanberry's relationship with his daughter strengthened. Though servants were available day and night, he insisted on tending to Aundrea when his wife was weak. The displeasure of having a girl waned with each smile and grip of his finger. When Dr. Wilshire returned a week later, it was if Mr. Galstanberry had transformed into a new man.

"Doctor, I have a few questions pertaining to Aundrea. Don't worry, it shall only take a moment." The doctor's eyebrow's rose in surprise. Mr. Galstanberry removed a piece of paper from his leather briefcase and then put on his spectacles. "Number one, when will Aundrea say her first word? Number two, how early can she start her schooling? Number three, what should her daily exercise regiment be? Number four, whe—"

"Mr. Galstanberry, please hand me the list. Perhaps, after I see…" When the list of twenty questions was placed in the doctor's hands, he immediately chuckled in surprise. "My goodness Charles!" Dr. Wilshire placed the list on the coffee table and began to check Mrs. Galstanberry's pulse, "I am glad your attitude has changed since my last visit!" Mr. Galstanberry nodded before interjecting, "Aundrea and I are getting along well. However, I am concerned about my Eleanor." The doctor's face grew solemn.

"Let's talk in the study."

Mrs. Galstanberry quickly sat up, "You-will-not! My body might be fragile, but," she coughed into a handkerchief and speckles of blood appeared, "I am emotionally and mentally capable. Do not treat me like a child!"

Dr. Wilshire sat on the bed and held her hands. "You have developed pneumonia—an inflammation of the lung." She closed her eyes to block the mournful gaze of the doctor and her husband's shocked expression. After a few minutes of silence, Mrs. Galstanberry gathered the strength to ask the question that anyone would dread asking, "How long?" She coughed harder, "How long do I have?"

"Due to your frail immune system and frequent illnesses, you have six months, perhaps a year." A tear rolled down her cheek as she nodded. "But, you are in the early stages. If the fever is kept down and your nutrition is good, you may have longer." Aundrea's cry startled everyone. It was as if she too, knew her mother's tragic fate. Mr. Galstanberry rocked the baby and then attempted to hand her to his wife. She instantly turned towards the window, while a fountain of tears soaked into her pillow. "Charles, I-I just can't right now." He held Aundrea tighter, "I understand, Eleanor. There will be other times." The weight of those words cut him like a knife.

• • •

In bed, Mrs. Galstanberry tried with all her might not to gaze out the window. The yearn to feel the warmth of the sun and to inhale the fresh, wild air was painful.

"Come on arms, help-me-up! Legs, work with me!" Out of frustration, she snatched a purple notebook from her bed stand and stared at it blankly.

What good will you do me?

A tear fell when her eyes drifted to Aundrea's crib. Immediately, she shook her head and straightened her back.

No, Eleanor, there's no time for tears!
You must be strong for Aundrea and Charles.

As she stared once more at the purple cover, an idea sprung to mind.

I may not be present all of Aundrea's life,
but my words will.

She urgently opened the first page and wrote a dedication in perfect calligraphy.

• • •

For the next few months, Mrs. Galstanberry sipped mint tea in bed and wrote the Memory Manual for Aundrea. It contained life lessons along with amusing anecdotes of her teenage and young adult years. "Almost finished?" Dr. Wilshire inquired as he entered the room for one of her bimonthly checkups. She smiled and closed the notebook, "How can one describe their entire life in a set of pages?" He laughed, "Certainly, it's easier than tilling soil and planting flowers for the rose garden." She winced as the needle poked her skin. "That is true, doctor; however, it is still a challenge." Mrs. Galstanberry wiped a tear away as she continued, "I want Aundrea to understand me; a mother she'll perhaps never truly know." He placed a band-aid on her arm and handed her a glass of water, "Eleanor, I admire your strength."

• • •

After seven months, Mrs. Galstanberry's health rapidly deteriorated. On August 1, 1927, her frail immune system could no longer battle pneumonia. At the funeral service, Mr. Galstanberry stood among weeping relatives, yet didn't shed one tear. As the preacher delivered the eulogy, the grief stricken husband could only think about the beauty and warmth his wife radiated at Aundrea's first birthday. A slow smile spread across his lips, as he remembered spreading cake frosting on Eleanor's nose, after blowing out their daughter's first candle together.

When Mr. Galstanberry returned from the service, he no longer look at Aundrea without crying uncontrollably. She shared his wife's infectious smile and sparkling eyes.

To cope with this immense grief, he labored at his company from the break of dawn to midnight. Unbeknownst to him, this would change very soon.

One gray, stormy day, Aundrea had an unusual crying fit. Perhaps it was the dreary weather, normal infant behavior, or fate beckoning father and daughter together. Regardless, Dr. Wilshire tried everything to soothe her—warm milk, hot bath and back rubs. To his dismay, nothing worked. It was now time to alert her father. At noon, Mr. Galstanberry stormed into the estate, "What is wrong?!"

The servant's knees shook as she answered, "Sir, M-Miss Aundrea wo-won't s-stop cr-crying. We have d-done e-everything!"

His eyes widened in anger, "You called me from my company for a baby's tantrum!? All of you should be fired for complete incompetence!!!"

Dr. Wilshire entered the room carrying a kicking, wailing infant, "There's no need for extreme measures. Your daughter has neither fever nor injury."

Mr. Galstanberry paced back and forth, "Then what is wrong! I have done everything for her! Everything!"

"Charles, calm down! If you hold her, I can fetch my stethoscope."

"No! No, I can't!"

"Of course, you can! You looked after her when Eleanor was ill." Mr. Galstanberry walked to the window and clasped his hands behind his back, "I haven't held her since the funeral."

"Sir, yo—"

"She doesn't need me, Henry! The servants can tend to her, they know what to do." Dr. Wilshire placed a hand on his shoulder, "It is YOU that is best for her." When he placed Aundrea in Mr. Galstanberry's arms, immense warmth filled his body. Within a few minutes, her crying and kicking ceased. "Raising her alone will not be easy. But Eleanor believed that you would be a superb father. And Charles, I believe that, too."

• • •

From that day forward, Mr. Galstanberry didn't schedule a business engagement without ensuring quality time with Aundrea. Although servants cared for her Monday through Friday, father and daughter were inseparable on the weekends. They picnicked by the pond on Saturdays and read nursery rhymes on Sundays.

As Aundrea grew older, they traveled to apple orchards, pumpkin patches, and museums. She inherited her father's chestnut curls, emerald eyes, and her mother's vivacious personality.

On the morning of her eleventh birthday, she excitedly pushed her French doors open and found three presents on the marble floor. One box was wrapped in pink paper, while the other two were wrapped in purple.

Just three?

"Faaather!" She screamed from the hallway.

Mr. Galstanberry shook his head in disapproval, "Aundrea, how many times must I tell you not to yell?"

"Whaaat?!"

He began ascending the stairs, "It is not proper for anyone, especially a young lady, to engage in conversation by shouting." She shrugged, completely oblivious to his complaint, "Are these it?"

"Excuse me?"

She thrust the gifts towards him, "Only three?"

"Don't you mean 'thank you'?"

"Father, how can I say thank you when I don't know WHAT they are or IF there will be more?"

His eyes widened in shock and voice deepened with annoyance, "After you have dressed and completed breakfast, we will talk on the veranda. Please bring the gifts unopened."

Within an hour, her feet stepped onto the wood of the veranda. Still perturbed by his daughter's ungrateful attitude, Mr. Galstanberry maintained his gaze at the morning sun. She placed the gifts on a miniature table, straightened her dress, and then quietly sat down. "Aundrea, for the past eleven years, I have given you everything a father could give their child—horses, riding clothes, the best tutors, and dresses you protest to wear."

"I know father, but—"

"I am not finished and do not, I repeat, do not interrupt again. Please, open the pink box."

She unwrapped the bow and carefully tore the pink paper. "Aundrea, the dedication is on the first page. Please read it clearly and loudly." She took a deep breath. "To Aundrea Virginia Galstanberry; my joy, my heart. May you always follow your dreams, stand your ground, persevere through obstacles, and live without regret." She slowly closed the book and stared at it, "I-I didn't even know her." Their eyes met as he held her hands, "And that's why she wrote this. Your mother wanted you to learn about her through HER own words and no one else's. Now, open the purple boxes."

Aundrea removed a long strand of pearls and held it up to the sun. "Oooo, they're beautiful!"

"Your mother wore them on your first birthday. Her greatest wish, was for you to be academically prepared for any career you choose."

"That's why I have so many tutors, right?"

"Indeed, the best in Connecticut. However, I feel your mother would want me to do more."

"More? Like what?"

"Not every girl receives a great education like you. In fact, some may never go to school!" She laughed, "Father, you can't help every girl in the whole wide world!" He looked at her sternly, "Of course not Aundrea. But, one must try and do what they can to improve this world. That is what your mother would have wanted." He left her to sit on the veranda and ponder those last words.

• • •

Mr. Galstanberry took a second leave of absence from his company. Every day, hour, and minute was spent constructing the academy.

One summer evening, while Aundrea watched her father by her usual post on the stairs, he called out, "It is rude to stare." When she crouched down on the bottom step, it squeaked. "Aundrea, there is no need to hide." He turned from the desk and motioned her over.

"I was only making sure you were okay." She explained while cautiously walking towards him. "And why is that?"

Aundrea folded her arms and looked at him sternly. "You write all day and all night! I don't get it! What's the matter?!" He smiled and then pointed to a stack of folders, "These, my dear, are resumés of school teachers and university professors from around the country." Her eyes widened as she lifted papers from the stack, "That's a lot."

"Yes, too much for one person. Could you assist me?"

"Me? I'm only eleven!"

"And so will your classmates. I can think of no other person to advise me on the instructors for Galstanberry Academy."

She stepped back and whispered to herself, "Gal-stan-berry Academy?"

He leaned into the desk and lifted his eyebrows, "What say you, Aundrea Virginia Galstanberry?"

• • •

On November 1, 1937 the estate was brimming with women from across the United States. Father and daughter interviewed over thirty women for fifteen teaching and administrative positions. The day culminated with a buffet of exotic fruits, cheeses and meat in the Grand Dining Hall. Mr. Galstanberry stood at the head of a long mahogany table, "Thank you again for interviewing for a staff position at Galstanberry Girls Academy. The school is a personal tribute to my wife, Eleanor Virginia Galstanberry." He smiled at his daughter, who sat with her hands folded properly in her lap. "My wife died of pneumonia after our daughter Aundrea's first birthday. Eleanor's greatest wishes for her daughter are incorporated into the Galstanberry motto. Aundrea, will you do the honor?" She nervously stood and surveyed the faces in the room. With her eyes closed, she recited from the heart.

"May all Galstanberry Girls pursue their dreams, stand their ground, persevere through obstacles and live without regret."

Her father raised a glass of sparkling red wine and declared with great pride, "To Eleanor!"

• • •

August 1, 2010

Dear Applicant:

The Admissions Council of Galstanberry Girls Academy would like to enthusiastically extend an offer of acceptance for the entering 2010 class. Your essay, grades and extracurricular activities distinguished you from a very competitive applicant pool. Delight in this accomplishment, but remember significant work still lies ahead.

Our Galstanberry graduates are extraordinary young ladies that have changed their communities with intelligence, creativity and integrity. A budding poet, accomplished equestrian, B-girl, ballet dancer and skilled debater are among your new class mates.

Embrace this opportunity, for it is just the beginning of tremendous achievements to come.

Welcome to Galstanberry Girls Academy!

Sincerely,

Victoria Galstanberry-Tissel

Headmistress Victoria Galstanberry-Tissel

Bronx, New York

August 5, 2010

Diario Mio[1]:

*Sheesh! Subways are soo noisy and rickety.
And privacy, what privacy? It's New York! I bet
the guy next to me is tryin to see this. Okay, no
more distractions. I have good, NO, <u>fantastic</u> news!
This morning I ripped open a thick envelope from
Galstanberry. And guess what?! I, Lillian Maria
Garcia, will be a Galstanberry girl! Can't wait to
tell my girls at the Puertorriqueño[2] parade Sunday!!*

*BUT, don't know how to feel. I mean, ½ of me is
excited, but the other ½ is really, REALLY nervous.
Could I flunk out? ¡Dios mio[3]! I'm gonna have a
panic attack and the cute guy will remember the
muchacha loca[4] that lost her cool. Okay, uno, dos,
tres[5]. Breath in, breath out. Gotta go, my stop's up.*

Will update soon!!

¡Adios[6]!
Lilly

---

[1] My diary; [2] Puerto Rican; [3] My God!; [4] Crazy girl; [5] 1,2,3; [6] Bye

Lillian

Sunday, August 29, 2010

"Bless me, Fawtha, for I have sinned. My last confession was, um, two weeks ago," Lillian stated in a thick New Yawk accent. She folded her hands and bowed her head. It was time to lay it all on the line—a complete admission of guilt. The confessional booth was dark and sufficiently serene that one could hear a pin drop. Unlike her rambunctious apartment, she could actually think here.

"Yes my child, proceed." Lillian breathed deeply and declared, "I lied to my sister, Maria."

Wow, that wasn't too painful.
I'll survive this—hopefully.

She relaxed her hands and stretched a little. "We were shoppin' in Manhatt'in and found this boutique in Soho with the ka-utest outfits—like bags, skirts, hoodies. Anyway, Maria found this frilly dress for her and Fernando's second year anniversary. When she asked my opinion, I told her she looked fat. Awright, awright, I said huge. Before I knew it, she was cryin', and we're on the next R train back home! We didn't tawk the en-ti-ire time."

Lillian paused and remorsefully continued, "I should've known beddah." Her eyes scanned the booth's ceiling for answers. "Well, she just had Luis, my cute new nephew. And now, she's all worried about her weight."

"What prompted you to insult her?"

"The whole trip she was tawkin' on-'n-on about how Gawlstanberry is good for me."

"It is! Galstanberry is an outstanding school! Only the best of the be—"

"Yea, yea, I know!"

"A tremendous blessing has come your way!"

"Blessing or curse?! Since opening that stupid leddah, I've transformed from 'lovable Lillian' to 'Lillian the liyah'!"

The priest cleared his throat, indicating strong disapproval. Lillian pursed her lips and went on, "There's more..."

"More?"

"Yeeaa. I lied to my dad, too." She hunched down, squeezed her eyes shut, and waited to be struck by lightning. After a minute, she sat up and continued, "I told him I couldn't work in his stawre because I was sick."

"But, you weren't sick?"

"Nope. Once I leave for Gawlstanberry, I won't be able to hang with my girls." Suddenly, a rush of panic overcame Lillian. "I won't see my parents,brothers,orsisters. Theymightforgetaboutme! Everyonemightforgetaboutme!"

"Slow down, my child, slooow doooown!" The priest used a handkerchief to wipe the sweat from his forehead. On the opposite side of the screen, Lillian nervously twisted a finger around her chocolate curls. Was she beyond redemption?

"First, you must trust God's plan. He has blessed you with a wonderful opportunity. Second, tell the truth. Whenever you feel compelled to lie, stop, and ask God for guidance." Lillian listened intently, trying to ignore the phone vibrating in her purse.

"Everyone makes mistakes. But it's our job, yours and mine, to acknowledge them." She nodded although her mind was trying to figure out the missed call. "Um, yes, Fawtha. Thanks, thanks a lot!"

Lillian pushed the velvet curtain aside and flipped her phone open.

MOM: Lilly donde estas?[7]
PAPI: Come home!
CARLOS: Me & E planning ur funeral!
EMILIO: Get home fast!
CAMILLA: What r u wearing 2 parade?
JALISSA: Will Carlos b there?

---

[7] Where are you?

Sheesh! Gone for like 15 minutes and the fam
acts like the world stopped spinnin!

She didn't think confessional would take so long. But hey, there was much to discuss. Her fingers texted back, "I'm k", and her eyes gazed at St. Paul's Cathedral's gothic architecture. The vaulted ceilings and stained glass windows added a majestic touch.

I've never noticed how incredible this place is.
Gonna miss it all.

The phone vibrated again.

Yea, yea, I'm comin'!

• • •

In the subway car, people stood shoulder to shoulder, and back to back—any movement was virtually impossible. To compound the already inconvenient situation, it was excruciatingly hot. Surprisingly, Lillian wasn't annoyed this time. She was actually going to miss standing awkwardly close to strangers, seeing kids' laugh when the subway lurched forward and listening to the stories of elderly women. Don't forget the cute guy sightings!

"Fowty-fawrth and Hawmilton. Transfah fawr the

R train hea." The conductor announced over the scratchy train speakers.

"Yikes, my stop! ¡Perdóneme[8], por favor[9]! ¡Per-dón-e-me!" She squeezed through people and escaped just before the doors closed. The familiar sounds of salsa music and hip-hop blared from cars as she exited the station. A multitude of Spanish voices rung like bells in her ears. For a couple of minutes, Lillian stood on the sidewalk jotting down ideas for a poem that would capture the street's bustling activity. As she began to walk down Hamilton Street towards Whitfields, her family's apartment complex, childhood memories sprung to mind.

She looked to her left and spotted the fire hydrant she tripped over while racing with friends. Across the street at Riviera Park, boys dripping with sweat earnestly played soccer. Restaurants like Julio's, which served delicious enchiladas, or Café Azul[10], renowned for its hot chocolate, illuminated the block with eye catching orange and yellow awnings. Emilio's Barber Shop, popular among neighborhood boys and her brothers, was next door to Deluxe Dulce[11], everyone's favorite candy store. She tilted her head up and smiled at the Puerto Rican flags that delicately waved from fire escapes. "¡Lo siento[12], Lo siento!" A group of kids shouted as they bumped her on their way to Armando's Ice Cream Parlor.

[8] Excuse me; [9] Please; [10] Blue Cafe; [11] Candy; [12] I'm sorry!

Her phone beeped once more.

> **MOM:** Lillian, venaca ahora mismo![13]

Whenever her mother used Lillian instead of Lilly, trouble was definitely ahead. She immediately ran down the block, rushed into Whitfields, and pressed seven in the elevator. She tiptoed down the hall and before her key turned in the lock, the door swung open.

• • •

Mrs. Garcia stood with fire brimming in her eyes. ¡Hola[14], Mamá[15]!" She attempted a hug, but her mother was stiff as a board. Her older brothers Carlos, eighteen, and Emilio, seventeen, quietly exited the apartment; glad to avoid their mother's wrath. "Mamá, Carlos and I are going to the stawre to help Papá move the float." She nodded with eyes fixed on her daughter. Lillian took a deep breath and slowly eased into the apartment. Mrs. Garcia made a slight pivot towards her, as if glued to the carpet. "Confession was helpful. I got a lot of things off my chest—I'm one-hundred percent beddah." She released a sigh as fake as the designer bags on Canal Street.

[13] Come home right now!; [14] Hello; [15] Mom

"Really? Did you apologize to your Fawtha for lying about being sick?"

¡¿Qué[16]?! How'd she know?

"Camilla's mom told me you were at their house. You were supposed to be working at the stawre!" Mrs. Garcia folded her arms.

"No, I haven't talked to Papí yet." She looked down at the floor and shuffled her feet nervously.

"Your Fawtha and I don't think you should go to Gawlstanberry tomorrow!"

"What?!"

"That's right! Your behavior these past weeks has been terrible. You cawl Maria fat knowing she's sensitive about her weight, and then lie to your Fawtha! What's going on with you?"

Lillian refrained from a response.

Maybe if I don't say anything…

"Lillian Maria Garcia, answer me!"

Uh oh, holding it in, hold it in! Too late.

"I'm afraid!" Tears streamed down her cheeks.

[16] What?

"Afraid? Afraid of what?! Is there anything else you need to say?"

"Mama, I—"

"What have you done, Lillian?! She shook her head while anxiously pacing the carpet.

"I'm afraid of Gawlstanberry!" Mrs. Garcia halted and looked at her daughter in shock. "Gawlstanberry? ¿Por qué[17]?" Lillian dramatically plopped on the couch and reached for the tissue box. "I'm gonna be away from you, Papí, everyone!" She blew her nose. "What if no one likes me? Or, if I flunk out?" Mrs. Garcia sat along side Lillian and held her hands. "My Lilly, my drama queen. Every student in your school, and probably the Bronx, would love to be in your place! I'm not sayin' schools here aren't good, but Lilly, you'll have the best—the best! Do you know what that means?" Lillian shook her head.

"World class teachers, rigorous curriculum, and more opportunities to spread your wings. And flunk out!? You get nothin' but A's! You deserve to be a Gawlstanberry girl!"

Lillian's eyes plead for forgiveness when she stated with great sincerity, "I'm so sorry, really I am." Mrs. Garcia shook her head, then stood. "Well, it's not ovah. You must apologize to your Fawtha and ask permission to participate in the parade. ¿Me entiendes[18]?" Lillian solemnly nodded.

• • •

[17] Why?; [18] Do you understand me?

Once again she walked down Hamilton, but now, every step was incredibly painful. The green-striped awning with *Garcia's Groceries* imprinted in gold writing drew near with each nervous breath. Once in the store she gulped.

Mrs. Rosario, a family friend greeted her with arms open. While hugging, Lillian's eyes searched the store for her father.

Wea is he?

"Y'excited about the parade? Everyone looks faw-wahd to seeing the float.

"Um, what?"

"Your Fawtha always has the best ideas!" Lillian didn't want to be rude, but she wasn't in the mood for conversation. "I'm sorry Señora[19] Rosario, but, I gotta go!" She hastily moved into Aisle Two and, at once, caught Emilio's eye.

Great! He's just gonna rub it in.

"E, where's Papí?" He looked her up and down. "In the back, waitin' for ya!"

"Whateva!" She replied while rolling her eyes and pushing the backroom's curtain aside. Her legs drudgingly walked the long corridor until a strange figure emerged.

[19]Mrs.

Standing almost as tall as the ceiling, was a huge chocolate flan intricately decorated with fruits.

Papí does have the best ideas!

Light green kiwi served as the bottom layer, while blueberries and raspberries filled the middle. Bright red strawberries, with white flakes to simulate sugar, topped the masterpiece. Lillian walked around the flan with her jaws dropped.

"That's exactly the reaction I was looking fawr!"

"Papí, this is fan-tastic! Good enough to eat!"

He laughed and sat at his desk.

Yes! Got him in a good mood!

"Can we, um, talk about yesterday?"

He nodded and motioned for her to sit.

Lillian's lips began to quiver. "So, I wasn't sick."

"Oh, you weren't?" His face didn't look too surprised.

"No, I-I just wanted to hang with Camilla and Jalissa."

"Lilly, you have your whole life to be with them. What's the rush?"

"Since I'm going to Gawlstanberry, I won't see them anymore!" She started speed talking again, "Maybethey'll forgetaboutme. Youandmommightforgetaboutme!"

"¿Como[20]? Cálmate[21] Lilly! We couldn't forget you, even if we tried." He winked. "Look, you'll be fine. Although me and your mom will be faw away, we're not gone faw-evah. We love you and expect to be treated with respect."

That's my cue. Here it goes.

"I'm really sorry, Papí, for lying to you and makin' fun of Maria. I didn't mean to disrespect anyone." As they hugged, his prickly beard tickled her forehead.

Gonna miss this, too.

"Alright, Lily, no more tears and stop being afraid. Go home and get dressed for the parade."

"I can go?"

"¡Sí[22], Por qué no[23]! The float wouldn't be the same without you!" She hugged him once more, and then rushed out the store. While running, she tried to steady the phone as it bumped her ear. "Chica, you haven't returned any of my calls! ¿Qué pasó[24]?"

Lillian sighed. It was like she was apologizing to everyone. "¡Lo siento, Jalissa! I had family stuff. You're still comin' to my apartment for the parade right?"

"¡Por supuesto[25]! Me and Camilla. What colors should we wea?"

[20] What?; [21] Calm Yourself!; [22] Yes; [23] Why not?; [24] What happened?; [25] Of course

"Wea red to match the strawberries."
"Ahh! ¡Adiós!

• • •

Lillian belly-flopped onto her emerald bed spread. "I should've gawn shopping!" She complained while burying her face into the bedazzled pillow. "Why, Lilly? You have the most clothes than any girl in the Bronx, probably Manhatt'in, too!" Camilla cautiously walked into the room and stepped over clothes like they were land mines. Lillian sat up and was on the brink of another complaint until she saw Camilla's red ensemble. "Wait-a-minute, you look good. Miiii-guel will be happy!"

"Don't even stawt, Lilly! You want to look good for An-tho-ny!"

"Who's An-tho-ny?" Mrs. Garcia teased with a Rue21 bag dangling from her fingers. "And why is this room so messy?" Camilla instantly began folding clothes, while Lillian ran to place dresses on hangers. Mrs. Garcia smiled approvingly and handed Lillian the bag.

"What?! You and Papí are already spendin' money for Gawlstanberry." She unraveled the tissue paper and gasped. "It's too cute!" The cherry sundress had puffy sleeves with violet flowers embroidered around the V-neck collar. Her mother pulled out a tiny, gold locket.

Inside was a picture of the entire family: Mr. and Mrs. Garcia, Maria, Emilio, Carlos and Lillian. "Since it's your last day hea, your fawtha and I wanted to give somethin' special."

"¡Qué bonita²⁶!" Jalissa exclaimed as she walked into the room. She twirled the locket around and nodded approvingly. "Good taste, Mrs. Garcia!"

"Thank you, Jalissa. Now, you girls beddah hurry up. The parade starts soon!" When she left, Lillian held the dress to her figure. "It's crazy, right?" The girls nodded in agreement. "Ahh!! I can't wait to wea it! So, while I change, Camilla, can you hang up my skirts? And Jalissa, could you put the jeans in the dresser?"

"You owe us Lilly!" Camilla said as she separated skirts from dresses.

When Lillian left, Jalissa stopped folding. "Awright, how do you really feel about her leavin'?" Camilla put a dress down. "I'm happy fawr her, ya know. It's just…"

"You don't want her to forget about us, right?"

"Yea."

The room suddenly got quiet when Lillian returned. "Is somethin's goin' on?" The two girls didn't respond. "Did I miss somethin'?"

Jalissa shrugged her shoulders. "Nothin." Lillian sighed and rolled her eyes. "Nothin', yea, whateva." Camilla closed one of the drawers and sat on the bed.

²⁶ How pretty!

"Look, me and Jalissa are gonna miss you, that's all. Lillian put her arms around both girls' shoulders. "C'mon. None of the girls at Gawlstanberry can even come close to my Bronx besties."

"For real?" Jalissa asked.

"For real, for real!" Lillian confirmed. The three finished organizing the room, primped their hair, and left for the parade.

• • •

Thousands of people crowded both sides of Hamilton. Mr. Garcia approached the girls with baskets. "Right on time! You'll be passin' out flyers that have a twenty percent off coupon. It can be used on anything in the stawre. Emilio will be driving a little fast, so walk quickly. If you get tired, just jump in the caw. There's a cooler in the backseat. ¡Buena suerte!"[27]

Mr. Rivera, director of the parade, straightened his back and spoke into the megaphone. "Okay, people, get your floats ready. We stawt in two minutes! Two minutes!"

The girls exchanged looks of excitement. "Yo, Lilly, you ready?" Emilio asked while admiring his new aviators in the side mirror.

"Puh-leeze, E, I was born ready!" As the drum rolls began, an Army officer walked from the rear of the parade

[27] Good luck!

to the front. "Ahh-ten-tion!" Four lines of soldiers marched in beige boots and black berets. Carlos carried the American flag and winked at Lillian as he passed their father's float.

The Rosemary High School marching band, elaborately dressed in red and blue, the colors of the Puerto Rican flag, followed close behind. One by one, floats were greeted by loud cheers. As Lillian neared the crowd, she began to panic.

What if people don't cheer? What do I do?

She began to shake and walk strangely from side to side, until Jalissa grabbed her arm. "Girl, snap out of it! Everything's gonna be fine. We're gettin' close, get your flyers ready!"

I can do this. I can do this.
Uno, dos, tres.
Breath in, breath out.

The crowd erupted like a volcano when the float appeared. While people piled on top of each other to see, the girls rapidly passed out flyers. "They love it!" Lillian yelled to Camilla.

"¿Como?"

"I said!" She took a bigger breath. "They love it!"

Camilla shook her head—it was impossible to

communicate over the noise. As the parade turned onto Verset Street, the girls climbed into the car to catch their breaths.

"This is what I'm gonna miss."

Jalissa squeezed her arm. "We'll be hea when you get back." The girls continued to pass out flyers until they reached Grivielle Street, the end of the route. There, Mr. Garcia greeted the group.

"Papí, they loved the float!"

"Sí, les escuché[28]! Me and your brothers are gonna return the float. Be home at five for dinner."

She shooed him away. "Yea, yea! I'll be on time!"

When Mr. Garcia left, Jalissa nudged Lillian. "Soooo, are you gonna say goodbye to An-tho-ny?"

Camilla puckered her lips. "A goodbye kiss after the poetry slam?"

Lillian laughed and rolled her eyes.

• • •

The girls walked around the parade and visited booths. People showed their cultural pride by wearing shirts with pavas[29], coquís[30], and other national insignia. After the girls finished eating, they walked towards the Pepsi music stage. "Lilly, I can't believe you're gonna do this." Jalissa hit Camilla's arm. "Don't make her nervous!"

[28] I heard them!; [29] Straw hats; [30] Tree frog that lives in Puerto Rico

¡Estoy loca![31] ¿Por que estoy haciendo esto?[32]

"Camilla, you're right! I'm gonna go and drop out!" When she began to walk away, Jalissa caught her arm, "Lilly, you write poetry all the time. Now, you gotta show it off!" She then turned to Camilla. "I told you not to scare her!" Lillian's mind was made up, or was it? "I'll be back." As she walked away, Camilla yelled, "Don't do it! I'm sorrrry!"

Lillian approached a short woman writing on a clipboard, while tapping her left foot impatiently. "Hello, Mrs. Sanchez!"

"Oh, hello, Lilly! I was excited to see your name on the slam roster."

"Riiiight, about that—"

"Your Mother tawks about your writin' all the time!

"She does?"

"¡Sí! She and your Fawtha are real proud."

Mrs. Sanchez stopped. "Oh, I'm sorry, we're you tryin' to say somethin'? You know I can go on-'n-on." She shook her head, unable to speak. "Awright, just listen for your name." Lillian returned to her friends in a daze.

"Ready to go home?" Jalissa asked as she crossed her fingers hoping the answer was no. "I-I can't. I gotta say my poem."

[31] I am crazy!; [32] Why am I doing this?

Suddenly, Jalissa's hazel eyes widened. "Lilly, Camilla, do NOT turn around. Anthony, Miguel, and Luis just sat in the front row."

"Where?" Camilla whispered as she looked from side to side. Jalissa rolled her eyes. "You'll just give us away, like always!"

"Fine!" Camilla knew being discreet wasn't her forte. The girls quietly sat three rows behind Anthony and his crew

• • •

"My name is Mrs. Lola Sanchez and I'm the chair of the parade's youth committee. Today, kids from the Bronx will use poetry to express themselves creatively. In the spirit of a slam, please snap your fingers after each performer. ¡No aplauda![33]" She looked down at her clipboard. "The first poet will be mi hijo[34] Mario Sanchez." He rolled his eyes in annoyance then began his poem. After ten performers, Lillian started to think that her name had magically (and fortunately) disappeared from the list.

"Lillian Garcia? Lillian Garcia?" Mrs. Sanchez called out repeatedly.

"What?! I'm not ready!"

---

[33] No applause!; [34] My son

When she slid down in her seat, Jalissa immediately stood and shouted repeatedly, "¡Lilly está aquí![35] ¡Lilly está aquí!"

Mrs. Sanchez looked into the audience and then smiled. "There you are, Lilly! Come to the mic!"

She rose slowly, tucked an orange notebook under her arm, and walked onto the stage. Her fingers trembled as she searched for a poem marked with a star.

"My poem is called. Um…it's called." She turned with her back facing the audience and squeezed her eyes shut.

You can do this. You…can..do this!
Uno, dos, tres.
Breath in, breath out.

"Go Lilly!" A deep, yet familiar voice shouted. When she faced the crowd, a tall, curly haired boy wearing a blue NY cap and Sean John polo, stood proudly. She gripped the microphone and nervously stated, "Um, my poem is called 'The Boogie Down Bronx." People bobbed their heads as each stanza was read. When she reached the last line, she closed the notebook and stated with immense pride,

[35] She is here!

"And that is why,
I can't deny,
The boogie,
The boogie down Bronx"

A chorus of finger snaps filled the air. "You were great, chica!" Jalissa whispered as Lillian returned to her seat. "Thanks, but I gotta meet the fam for dinner." The girls snuck out and stood by a light post.

"This block won't be same without you," Camilla quietly remarked through sniffles. "Uh oh, here goes water works." Jalissa teased as she put her arm around Lillian's shoulders. "Cawl us when you get there, kay? So this one." She pointed to Camilla. "Won't go loca!"

As the three hugged for the last time, Lillian's phone beeped.

| **MOM:** B home by 5 Lilly! |

"Yikes, gotta go!"

• • •

As Lillian walked through her apartment door, Maria looked up from playing with Luis.

"Hola, Lilly!"

"Um, hey, Maria…" She sat down at the opposite end of the couch. After a few minutes, Lillian moved closer to her sister. "I'm really sorry for sayin' you looked huge." Maria shook her head. "No, I shouldn't have bothered you about Gawlstanberry."

Mrs. Garcia emerged from the kitchen and wiped her flour-drenched hands on the apron. "Lilly! You, Camilla, and Jalissa were fan-tastic! Did you have fun?"

"Yea, but—"

"Your Fawtha cawld and said the crowd was chee—"

"Mamá! Maria and I are tawkin' hea!"

She promptly returned to the kitchen, thankful that her daughters were speaking again.

Lillian smiled at Luis playing on her sister's lap. "Can I hold him?" Maria nodded and began to place plates and silverware on the table. "Lilly, when I left for college, I was nervous, too."

"Really? You seemed happy!"

"¡Por supuesto! But scared-to-death! Would I fit in? Will I get good grades like in high school? My mind was like spinnin'!" She returned to the couch and tickled Luis' feet. "But I dropped that fear when I thought of all the possibilities. I could major in psychology and study in another country. Basically, I could accomplish anything I wanted!" Lillian handed Luis back. "Once I embraced all the possibilities, I didn't have time to be scared."

The moment Mrs. Garcia placed the roasted chicken on the dining room table, Carlos, Emilio, and Mr. Garcia rushed through the door, and of course, towards the delicious aroma. As everyone dug into the food, Lillian spoke up, "Carlos, are you excited about leavin' tomorrow?" Everyone stopped eating mid bite.

¡Ay! Why did I say that?

She tried to smooth things over, "Afghanistan. Sounds exciting, right? I'd love to visit another country." Mrs. Garcia frowned and shot up from the table. "I'll get the lemonade."

Mr. Garcia squeezed Emilio's shoulder. "There's no greater honor than servin' your country. And don't you forget that!" Mrs. Garcia placed the pitcher on the table and slowly sat down. "Carlos, I love you. You know that right?"

"¡Por supuesto, Mamá!" She blinked her eyes to clear the tears. "But every time I watch the news or hear the doorbell ring, I can't help but think the worst!"

Mr. Garcia cleared his throat. "Gloria, not now." She shook her head. "¿Por qué no, Fernando? Let me speak my mind!" His protest ceased. "The day you signed up I cried."

"Mamá, I didn't kn—"

"You were eighteen, I couldn't stop you. And when you walked out that door, I didn't eat or sleep for days!"

She paused, then smoothed her hair down.

"Don't worry, I'm beddah now. But remember, you might be a soldier out there." She pointed to the window. "¡Pero, eres mi hijo aquí![36] ¿Me entiendes?" When Emilio rushed to hug his mother, Lillian joined in. "Te quiero[37] Carlos!" He lifted her from the ground and kissed her cheek. "I love you, too, Lilly!"

Mr. Garcia clapped his hands. "Okay, okay, time for dulce de papaya![38]"

The family enjoyed dessert, and most importantly, a moment in which all of them were together.

• • •

In Lillian's room, the sisters shifted through green suitcases. "Do you have toothbrushes, tooth paste, and towels?"

"Yes, yes, and yes!"

Maria checked those items off the list. "It also says six binders, pencils, and paper." Lillian pointed to a stack of school supplies. "Got those, too!"

"And outfits for Fridays?"

"Yep! I'll be the ka-utest girl there!"

Mrs. Garcia leaned against Lillian's desk and checked her watch. "Is she done?"

[36] But, you are my son, here!; [37] I love you! [38] Bread custard

Maria nodded, and then suddenly hugged Lillian. Mrs. Garcia wrapped her arms around the both of them.

"I'll be fine, for real!" But, they didn't loosen their grip. "Ay! You're gonna hug me to death!"

"Lilly! Liiiiilly! A boy's here to see you!" Carlos yelled from the living room.

Boy? For me?

• • •

Anthony stood with his hands in his jeans' pockets. Mrs. Garcia entered the living room with her eyebrows raised in surprise. "Anthony, your visit is a little late."

"Yes Mrs. Garcia, but Lilly left the slam before I could congratulate her." Carlos slapped Anthony's back, causing him to stumble. "What up, man?"

"Nothin', just waitin' for school to stawt. You're leavin' tomorrow too, right?" Emilio stepped forward and looked Anthony up and down. "Yea, he is. But, I'm still gonna be watchin' Lilly." Mr. Garcia shooed the brothers to their rooms, then grabbed Luis' diaper bag and followed Maria out of the door. When the living room finally emptied, Anthony and Lillian stared at each other in silence.

"Wanna sit?"

"Yea, thanks." She sat beside him with her hands folded and legs crossed at the ankles.

"Anthony, want some water?" He shook his head. "Naw. I'm okay."

"Sooo, did you have fun at the parade?" He didn't answer.

If he's not goin' to tawk, why's he hea?

"Anthony? An-tho-ny?" He turned to her. "I'm just thinkin' of what to say."

"Ookay…" She quietly mumbled.

"So, your poem was really good. How'd you come up with it?"

"I'll be right back!" She ran from the room and grabbed a shoebox from the top rack of her closet. When she returned, she placed it on the dining room table. "Lilly, why is 'TOP SECRET' written on it?"

"'Cause it is!" She removed an orange notebook and started to flip through the pages. "I take this everywhere."

"Why?"

"Everything inspires me to write. Ridin' the subway, walkin' on Hamilton, even helpin' people in my dad's stawre." She pointed to a page with a sketch of an ice cream cone. "This one's about some niñas[39] I saw laughin' and eatin' at Armando's." She flipped more pages. "Oh, and

[39] little girls

this one talks about Luis."

Anthony smiled. "As you were readin' the poem, I realized why that school chose you." She blushed. "But I gotta be honest, I'm not really happy you're leavin'. Wait! That didn't sound right." The two once again sat in silence. "I'm happy you're gettin' a good education and all. But, aren't you scared, Lilly?"

"Yea, until I tawked to Maria. She was scared to leave him, too."

"Really?"

"She didn't know if her college classes would be too hard, or if people would like her."

Anthony shook his head, "Whatcha worried about? You're the smartest girl in our class." He leaned into the table. "I know you're gonna be like a lawyer, doctor, or somethin' big." His smile made her twirl her finger around her curls. "Anyway, I gotta go. Mis padres[40] are gonna be mad if I come home too late, ya know." They both left the table and walked slowly to the door. "Thanks, Anthony, for comin'." Without thinking, she kissed his cheek.

"Um, adios, Lilly!" He bumped into the door, "Ouch!" Then ran down the hallway holding his forehead and waving goodbye. Mrs. Garcia emerged from the bedroom. "Sooo…What did An-tho-ny say?" Lillian fell onto the couch with her arms folded.

[40] My parents

"Just that I'm smart and nice. And basically everyone's gonna miss me."

"I believe that, don't you?"

"Yeaaa..."

"Then what's wrong?" Lillian played with the locket around her neck. "I'm not the only smart girl in the Bronx."

"Of course not."

"So, he'll probably find another girl to like. And because I'll be all the way in Connecticut, I won't even have a chance!"

Mrs. Garcia faked a serious expression to mask the smile trying to break through. "Lilly, there will always be someone prettier and smarter than you."

"That's not helpin'."

Mrs. Garcia shook her head. "But, there's only one Lillian Maria Garcia."

"You're right! He isn't going to find this," she pointed to herself, "Anywhere else!"

"That's the Lilly I love! Now, go-to-bed!"

• • •

Lillian hopped onto the bed and sat cross legged. She quietly laughed to herself while reading her phone's incoming messages.

> **CAMILLA:** Miss ya chica!
> **JALISSA:** Call us! Miss u girl!
> **MARIA:** Te quiero!

After texting back "Gracias!" she wrote in her diary:

Watch out Galstanberry!
Lillian Maria Garcia is comin'!

Atlanta, Georgia

August 10, 2010

Dear Diary,

I got in!!! Just call me Miss Galstanberry.
Yeah, I know, what's up with the cheesy name?
Personally, 'I looove the way it rolls off the tongue.
G-a-a-lstanberry. For real!

Say it the way people say H-a-a-rvard, which is the
college I'm going to because of G-a-a-lstanberry.
It's only the best school in the U-S-A. When I
graduate, the sky (better yet, the <u>stratosphere</u>) is
the limit!

Alright, that's the upside. The bad part is I have to
leave mom, dad, Tam, the twins, my homegirlz,
and sunny Atlanta for cold, and probably boring,
Connecticut. Don't get me wrong, I'm really ecstatic
about everything, just sad I have to leave. Yikes!
Gotta practice my elevés and solo for church!

Don't worry Diary, I won't leave you hangin.

Love,
Dee

Brandi

Sunday, August 29, 2010

"**M**iss Brandi, pay ah-tten-tion!" chastised Ms. Jones as she stretched her arms for second position. Her bun, which resembled a Christmas bulb at the top of a tree, shone in the studio lights. The black leotard and leopard skirt accentuated her Beyoncé curves. "Miss Amber, straight-ten those limp arms i-mmediately!"

Geez, someone's got an attitude today!

She rapped a stick on the nicely waxed wooden dance floor. "On my count! First position **<rap>**, second **<rap, rap>**, third **<rap, rap, rap>**, now demi-plié! Backs and shoulders straight, and to-the-front! Hold the pa-si-tionnn."

Brandi swallowed hard as Ms. Jones gracefully glided around the room straightening arms and scrutinizing stances. "Miss Nia, you call that a demi-plié? It looks like a demi-flop!" The class snickered.

"Do I hear laughter?"

"No, Ms. Jooonesss!" They replied in perfect unison.

"I thought so. Some of you look worse than her!"

The girls straightened their backs to avoid being the next victim.

Please, let her pass me! Please! Please!

Sweat poured down Brandi's neck as she strained to sustain the plié. Ms. Jones gave a nod of approval, and then walked to the front. "Everyone to the barre!"

Sighs of relief could be heard as girls sashayed to the long, wooden cylinder mounted to the wall. "Today, we practice elevés."

"Aww, man," said one girl.

"Not elevés!" Complained others.

Ms. Jones vigorously shook her head. "Girls, one must practice to be great! Not good, but grrr-ate! Now, face the barre! Feet, shoulder-length apart." She went down the line correcting each girl's feet.

"Dee, did you get in?" Amber whispered.

Brandi checked to make sure her instructor wasn't looking. "Yeah, I did."

Ms. Jones cleared her throat. "I should be the ONLY one talkin'. Now, e-le-vé!" Girls pressed up to the balls of their feet and lifted their heels off the floor. "Slowly rise to full-pointe and hold."

Amber's legs began to shake. "I ha-ate this part!"

Ms. Jones immediately stood behind her. "I said full-pointe, young lady. Up on those toes!"

Amber slowly rose. "Yes, Ms. Jo-oh-nesss." Brandi smiled to herself—ballet class would definitely be missed.

"Alright, girls, lower your heels." She returned to the front. "Many of you have asked why class was held Sunday morning instead of our usual Saturday class. So, Miss Brandi, please come to the front."

Me? What did I do?

She walked at a snail's pace, frequently looking back at her fellow dancers. "Vite[1]! Vite! We don't have all day!" Her legs instantly sped up. "Today is Miss Brandi's last day." Some girls dropped their jaws, while others put hands over their mouths. "This fall, she will be a pupil at the Galstanberry Girls Academy in Ka-ne-ti-cut. I have known Miss Brandi since she was dancing in size-two slippers and pink tutus."

The class giggled as Brandi looked at the floor. "Miss Brandi, pos-turrre, please!"

Her head shot back up. "Yes, ma'am!"

Ms. Jones walked to the studio's stereo system. "Is this the disc you brought?"

"Yep, I mean, yes Ms. Jooones."

"Good. Class, we will have free ballet dance to a song Brandi's selected. Every move must be ballet and—"

[1] Faster

"But, we dance ballet every Saturday! Can't we try somethin' else?" Amber pleaded with her hands clasped under her chin.

"Yeah! Yeah!" Chimed in her classmates.

Ms. Jones raised a hand for silence. "I am not finished. You may dance ballet and/or any PG-13 move." The room erupted in laughter, but Ms. Jones hushed the dancers before asking, "Are you ready?"

"Yeeeahh!!"

"Now, girls, get in pa-si-tionnn." As soon as Ms. Jones pressed play, a female voice sung out,

Leeeeet's get it started in heeeerre!!!

Ms. Jones immediately plugged her ears to block the screams. Her students' moves ranged from pliés, the robot, Soulja Boy, to Shakira hip-shaking. Once the chorus started, all shouted:

Let's get it started (Ha!),
Let's get it started in here.
Let's get it started (Ha!),
Let's get it started in here.
Yeah![2]

At the end of class, Brandi was overwhelmed with hugs and well-wishes. As she and her mother walked to the car, Nia shouted, "See you at afternoon service!"

• • •

[2] "Let's Get it Started," Black Eyed Peas

The Johnson house was positioned in the middle of the block with unmistakable dark purple bricks and a bright red door. The pristine peach trees that lined the cobblestone street were often suspected to be the source of Dr. Johnson's tantalizingly sweet peach cobbler. When the car pulled into the driveway, Brandi ran upstairs. She swung her door open and was stunned at the sight before her.

"Where's my blouse!?" Tamara, her sixteen-year-old sister, demanded as she tapped her foot.

What is she doing in my room?

"Don't act like you didn't hear me!" She stepped closer. "It's MY blouse; where is it? Moooom!!!!"

In the next room, Michael and Jamal laughed hysterically, and wiped away tears that streamed down their faces. "Mike, this is the best prank yet." Jamal said as he searched for tissue. "I know, Bro. We can't let Brandi leave without giving her a good memory of her baby bros." The Johnson trickster twins, a nickname coined by kids in the neighborhood, relished in seeing people squeal. Their neon-orange room was divided into two parts: living quarters with green bunkbeds; and the "Prank Factory" which came complete with its own sign, whoopee cushions, black mouth candy, fake cockroaches—you name it, they had it. Michael buttoned his navy dress suit and turned to Jamal. "Man, puttin' Tam's blouse in Brandi's dresser was per-fect."

"Yep, our genius can be imitated but NEVER duplicated." They high-fived and continued to get dressed.

• • •

Back in Brandi's room, the two sisters stared each other down. Brandi narrowed her eyes like a Siamese cat and crossed her arms. "Why would I even take your blouse?"

Tamara popped her collar and twirled in her dress. "Because, Lil' Sis, I have impec-cable fashion taste." She then flipped the bed's mattress, peered behind the computer, and tried to get inside the closet, but Brandi barricaded it, arms and legs stretched across the front. Tamara immediately sprinted to Brandi's dressers, threw open the first drawer and found exactly what she was looking for. "Ah HA! Here it is! Okay, Miss Brandi John-son, you have thirty-seconds to explain yourself. Make-it-quick!"

Brandi gathered her nerve and cautiously spoke, "Okay, Tam, I did borrow your necklace."

"My heart one?"

She nodded.

"Fine, keep talking."

"But, Tam, I have no, NO idea where your blouse is!"

Tamara's anger slowly faded when she realized the silliness of the situation. Her mother always said that imitation is the greatest form of flattery. "Brandi?"

"Yeeeah?"

"Look, sorry for accusing you. But you do take my stuff without askin'. Next time, just ask, alright?" Brandi smiled slyly.

I knew she'd back down.

• • •

In the bright-yellow kitchen, Dr. Johnson stirred grits and eyed the browning pancakes on the griddle, while Mr. Johnson searched for his glasses. "Honey, I told you the girls were going to work it out. If I ran upstairs every-single-time Tamara or Brandi called me, I'd go crazy!"

"Yep, dear, whatever you say." He scratched his head and searched the counter.

"They're next to the microwave, James." Dr. Johnson responded without turning her attention away from the stove.

"Michelle, what would I do without you?" Mr. Johnson teased as he kissed her cheek.

"Do you really want me to answer that?"

"Nope!"

"That's what I thought. Now, please tell the kids to hurry. Just because we're attending afternoon service, doesn't mean they can't get dressed in a timely fashion." Mr. Johnson nodded while ascending the stairs. He helped Michael and Jamal tie their ties; Brandi select the pink-striped sweater over the purple–polka-dotted; and convinced Tamara that blush, mascara, and lipstick were neither age appropriate nor necessary for church. After a late breakfast, the family piled into the car and headed to Olive Mount Baptist Church.

• • •

When Brandi's feet stepped across the church door's threshold, her heart beat quickened. "You'll be fine!" Her mother remarked after a comfort hug.

"Yea, Sis, you got this!" Michael chimed in, while Jamal nodded. Mr. Johnson squeezed Brandi's shoulder firmly and Tamara gave the 'you-go-girl' look. The family then dispersed: the girls went to the choral room, the twins carried their snares to the band hall, Mr. Johnson joined the ushers, and Dr. Johnson entered the sanctuary on a mission to find the perfect pew for her family. After Sister Andrews delivered announcements and tithes were collected, Pastor Jones approached the wooden pulpit. In a booming voice that echoed throughout the sanctuary, and even shook the stained glass windows, he greeted the congregation.

"Good morning, church! Isn't this beautiful weather a blessing?" All nodded. "Today is youth day, a time for the children to show off their extraordinary talent and most of all, their love for God. Our first selection is..." He looked down at a piece of paper. "'His Eye Is On the Sparrow,' performed by Miss Brandi Johnson, the Joyful Noise choir, and accompanied by the youth band." The choir took their positions on the risers as Brandi slowly approached the microphone. The band, including Jamal and Michael, settled behind their instruments.

Alright, I can do this!

She took a deep breath and begun.

"Why should I feel discouraged?
Why should the...should the..."

Her mind went completely blank.

I know this, I know this!

Nia ran to the microphone and smiled at the audience. "Just, uh, give us a minute." People looked at each other in confusion. She then whispered, "What's going on? Are you okay?" Brandi shook her head in response. "Girl, you have to pull it together! You got this, remember?" Brandi peeked over Nia's shoulder to search for her parent's faces. Before the first tear fell, a sparkle from Dr. Johnson's emerald brooch caught her eye.

There they are!

Brandi straightened her posture and spoke into the microphone, "I'm going to start from the beginning." She closed her eyes, opened her mouth, and sung out.

> *"Why should I feel discouraged?*
> *Why should the shadows come?*
> *Why should my heart feel lonely?"*

The choir hummed, while the band began to play.

> *"And long for heaven and home.*
> *When Jeeesus is my portion*
> *A constant friend is he.*
> *His eye is on the sparrow.*
> *And I know he watches over me.*
> *His eeeye is on the sparrow—"*

She paused dramatically,

> *"And I know he waaaatches meee."*

As her eyes opened, people stood on their feet, cheering and clapping enthusiastically. Pastor Jones cleared his throat and nodded with approval. "Our youth can accomplish anything when they put their mind to it! I would also like to extend extra congratulations to Miss Johnson for her acceptance into the Galstanberry Girls Academy."

After service, people waited in a long line to shake Brandi's hand and bestow words of wisdom. It was like being a celebrity, minus the annoying paparazzi. While the family walked back to the car, she took a nostalgic look at the church.

• • •

The Johnson's traditional Sunday dinner was transformed into Brandi's going away party. Her cousins, aunts, uncles, and the families of Nia and Amber were expected to come. Brandi secured the clasp of her teardrop necklace and twirled in the yellow flowered dress. She then wistfully walked around her pink room, admiring the furniture like it was newly purchased.

I'm gonna miss my life in Atlanta.

"You look cute!" Tamara remarked as she entered the bedroom.

"Thanks, Tam! Soooo, I've been thinking. If you didn't

hide the blouse and I definitely didn't do it. Who could?"

The girls looked at each other, then shouted, "The twins!"

Brandi laughed, "I don't know why we didn't think of them before!" Tamara shook her head, "Yea, they think their sooo slick! Payback's definitely a must!"

Brandi folded her arms and tilted her head to the side. "Remember when we used to act like we were famous movie actresses?"

"Yeah. I was Halle Berry and you were Nia Long."

"Right. Now, we can really put on a show!"

Tamara raised her eyebrows. "Dee, stop playin'! There's no Will Smith or Denzel Washington here!"

"I know! But at the party tonight, let's get into a big, Hollywood-style fight about the blouse. I'm talkin' full drama."

"Alright, and?"

"Well, Mom and Dad will pretend to be soo mad that they won't let me leave tomorrow."

Tamara laughed. "You're soo crazy! But, I'm down with idea! I'll go to the kitchen and put Mom in a good mood. Just finish getting dressed for your par-tay." Brandi nodded then searched her closet for the perfect sandals.

Yellow, to match my dress, or red?

As she modeled the red ones in the mirror, the irresistible smell of triple-cheese macaroni beckoned her downstairs. "Mm, mm, good! I know Galstanberry won't have food like this. So Mom, what about an itsy-bitsy bite?"

Dr. Johnson busily chopped potatoes, while Tamara washed peaches. "Brandi, your guests will be here in two hours, and food STILL needs to be made. There's no time to sample anything. Now, wash those apples before cutting them. And Brandi, please put on an apron this time! I don't want you to mess up another nice dress."

Tamara inched closer to her mother. "Mom, Brandi and I need to talk to you."

"Only if we can cook and talk. If not, then you girls must wait until after the party." Brandi tied the apron and turned on the faucet. She'd let Tamara take the lead. "Michael and Jamal put my blouse in Brandi's dresser so we'd fight!"

Dr. Johnson frowned and stopped chopping. "I'm sorry, girls. You know your Father and I don't tolerate that type of behavior. The boys will be punished after the party, trust me."

Brandi spoke up, "Tam and I were thinking about teaching them a lesson."

"That's noble of you both. What's the plan?"

Brandi moved closer. "We want you and Dad to be in on it."

Dr. Johnson placed the knife on the countertop and faced her daughters. "In on it?!"

Tamara quickly jumped in, "It's really not hard. Just be your mean self when one of us does something bad."

Dr. Johnson raised her eyebrows. "My mean self? Excuse me?"

Brandi hit her sister, and then led their mother to the kitchen table. "Mom, Tam didn't mean that."

"Oh, really? Why don't you girls try again? Just be careful this time."

Brandi sat down and folded her hands like a CEO presiding over a board meeting. "Tam and I will start arguing about the blouse. Our fight will get so bad that you and dad forbid me from going to Galstanberry tomorrow."

"And girls, when is this big performance supposed to occur?"

Brandi looked to Tamara, who cautiously answered, "Tonight, during Dad's toast..."

Dr. Johnson rapped her fingers against the table. "Fine, your father and I will do it."

"Yes!!!!!"

"But, under one condition."

Brandi leaned into the table. "Okay, what's that?"

"It's done tastefully. I don't want this production to end up on the six o'clock news. Understand?" The girls nodded excitedly. "Good, that's settled. Let's finish cleanin' and cookin'. Boooys!!!" The twins scuffled into the kitchen, trying to avoid the harsh glares from Brandi and Tamara. "The library, living and dining rooms need to be swept and vacuumed. And every piece of furniture in this house MUST be dusted."

"Aww, Mom!" They complained.

"Is there a problem boys?!"

Jamal hurried to the cupboard for dust cloths, while Michael immediately flipped the on switch of the vacuum cleaner.

<Ding, Dong>

Brandi rushed to the door, swung it open, and yelled excitedly, "Grandma Irene!"

"Hey, Suga!" She replied in a sweet Southern accent.

"Is that a new purse?" Brandi asked as she admired her grandmother's mustard-yellow CHANEL.

"Of course it is! Do you like?" They walked into the library and sat on the couches.

"Everything you wear is nice! Plus you're always matching!"

Grandma Irene pointed to her blazer. "It's CHANEL, too! But enough about me! Are you excited about leavin'?"

"Well, I think so…"

"You think so?!" Tamara repeated as she pushed

Brandi over for a spot on the couch.

"Oh hush, Tam, let the girl be!" Grandma Irene put her arms around Brandi's shoulders. "If you need me, just call anytime. You hear me? Any-time!" She then turned to Tamara, "And don't think you're too grown to call me, too!"

Dr. Johnson entered the room sipping a glass of orange juice. "Mom, can you help me in the kitchen? That is why you came early, right?"

"I guess I can show you a thing or two." Dr. Johnson gave the girls a 'yeah right' eye roll as she followed her mother. While Brandi returned to her room, Tamara flipped through records to find music for the party. She held Michael Jackson's Off the Wall album in the air and kissed it. "Muah!" As the needle touched the spinning Vinyl disc, a crackled noise was released. She tapped her toes to the opening verse and sung along with the chorus:

> *"Keep on with the force, don't stop*
> *Don't stop 'til you get enough*
> *Keep on with the force, don't stop*
> *Don't stop 'til you get enough"*[3]

\<Ding Dong, Ding Dong\>

[3] "Don't Stop Till You Get Enough," Michael Jackson

"I'm comin'!" Brandi yelled as her sandals flip-flopped down the stairs. Uncle Dave, Mr. Johnson's youngest brother, and his wife, Aunt Chandra, were the first to arrive.

"Congratulations!" Aunt Chandra greeted as she handed Brandi a small gift.

"I'd hug you, Auntie, but your baby bump…"

"Girl, give me a hug!" Aunt Chandra exclaimed as she pulled Brandi into her arms. Elijah, their ten-year-old son, squeezed between them and looked from left to right. "Where's Jamal and Mike?"

Brandi folded her arms. "I'm just invisible, huh?" She rolled her eyes then pointed to the ceiling. While racing up the stairs, he shouted, "Good joooob cuuz!!"

"So Brandi, what are you excited about most?" Uncle Dave asked as he helped his wife to the couch.

"The uniforms are soo cute!!"

Aunt Chandra laughed, "Sweetie, that can't be the only reason!"

<Ding Dong>

"No, it's n—"

<Ding Dong, Ding Dong>

"I-I'll be back in a sec!" When she swung the door open, a woman wearing a long, green dress smiled. "Hey, Aunt JoAnne! Where's Uncle William?"

She sighed and pointed to the driveway. "At the car, thinking of ways to carry everything." Before Brandi and her aunt could even make it back to the library…

<Ding Dong>

"I'm comin'! I'm comin'!"

This time, Brandi was almost knocked over when she opened the door. "Congrats, girl! You did it!"

"Nia, okay, okay! You can let go now!"

Her friend stepped back, "Oops! I almost forgot!" and lifted a sparkly green bag.

"Nia, you didn't have to!"

A short woman with a long, brown ponytail approached the girls. "Of course we had to get you something! But I don't want to interrupt you two. So, where's your mother Brandi?"

"She's in the kitchen, Ms. Sims, and thank you!"

Nia turned around when her mother disappeared around the corner. "Any calls from Jooo-ey?"

Brandi's heart beat began to race. "N-no, no-not yet." Suddenly, a red car beeped its horn and a girl ran up the porch towards them.

"Hey, peeps! Are you ready to par-tay?!"

Nia folded her arms. "Girl, I'm surprised you didn't show up until dessert!"

Amber let out an annoyed sigh. "Does fashionably late mean anything to y'all?"

Brandi shook her head as she locked the door. "Fashionably late? Girl, you're just late!"

• • •

In the library, Mr. Johnson cleared his throat to quiet the guests. "Thank you all for coming to celebrate Brandi's acceptance into Galstanberry. I hope everyone brought their appetite because we have ribs, potato salad, green beans and… Wait, am I making y'all hungry?" Everyone laughed. "Good! Let's start eatin'!"

Catfish, chicken, and ribs were in food warmers on the counter. The oven was decorated with bowls filled with triple-cheese macaroni, collard greens and black-eyed peas. Don't be shy! There's plenty of food!" Dr. Johnson yelled over the commotion.

Michael scooped a large chunk of potato salad onto Elijah's plate. "Man, whatcha doin', that's too much!"

Jamal put a hand on his cousin's shoulder. "Help some brothas out! If we have leftovers, then Mike and I have to eat this food for a year!"

"For real?" Elijah asked in astonishment.

Jamal nodded. "Yeah, man, no Mickey D's, Burger King, or Pizza Hut for a year!" Elijah nodded sympathetically, then scooped out more macaroni and cheese while the twins secretly high-fived each other.

People, plates, and paper cups were spread throughout the house. Everyone ate and tapped their toes to *Off the Wall*'s fifth track, "Workin' Day and Night." Before dessert, Mr. Johnson gathered all the guests once more into the library. "Again, I'd like to express my gratitude for your support this evening. As you all know, the economy is not doing well right now. Therefore, paying Galstanberry tuition is not a luxury. But my wife— Michelle, please come up here."

She walked to the front and held his hand. "But, Michelle and I believe that education is a worthy investment. We have three other children, a mortgage, bills—well, y'all know the story." The adults nodded with sympathy. "We know Brandi will work hard every day knowing the sacrifice we're making for her."

Tamara moved to the front of the room. "I think Brandi should make a speech."

"Yeah, go ahead!" Nia encouraged.

"That's right, speak, Suga!" Grandma Irene chimed in.

"Let me go first. As the older sister, I want to make sure Brandi does well. She shouldn't worry or have any distractions at Galstanberry." Tamara then turned towards her sister. "So, Brandi, please tell everyone how you stole my blouse."

"What is she talkin' about?" Nia whispered to Amber, who held a hand over her mouth in shock.

Brandi rushed to her sister's side, "Tam, not now!" Tamara folded her arms. "Just admit it!"

"Admit what!"

"That you're a no good thief!"

Brandi rolled her eyes. "I'm innocent until proven guilty! That's the LAW!"

"Oh, yeah? Then, you are guilty, guilty, GUILTY!"

"And why's that?"

Tamara stepped closer and pointed her finger in Brandi's face. "Because, MY blouse was in YOUR dresser. Explain that Miss Innocent!"

Everyone gasped, while Jamal and Michael exchanged nervous looks.

"Is this true?" Mr. Johnson asked.

"Well I-I..."

He removed the cell phone from his back pocket. "We can put a stop payment on your Galstanberry tuition check. All it takes is a phone call."

Michael nervously whispered to Jamal, "Man, we can't let Brandi go down like this."

Jamal hit his arm. "It's her or us!"

Brandi shook her head in desperation, "But Mom, Dad, I didn't take it, I proooomise!!"

"Brandi, your mother and I are so, so…" Instead of finishing, Mr. Johnson began pressing the numbers on the phone.

"It's not her fault!" Jamal shouted as Michael shook his head in defeat.

"Well, whose is it, Son?"

"Ours," Michael answered reluctantly. "It was only supposed to be a joke—a funny gift, ya know?"

Brandi glared at the twins. "No one's laughing."

Mrs. Johnson grabbed the arms of both boys. "We are going to your room to talk." She then turned to the guests, "Please, enjoy dessert! Don't let our misfit boys ruin the fun."

The group moved slowly, unsure of how to react. Sensing their uncertainty, Mr. Johnson clapped his hands together. "Folks, I present you my beautiful and brilliant actresses, Miss Tamara and Miss Brandi Johnson." The girls bowed, then gave each other high fives.

Amber shook her head, "So y'all were just acting?" The girls nodded. "And Mr. Johnson, you and Dr. Johnson knew the whole time?" He nodded and smiled. Amber folded her arms, and then smiled, "Can ya'll adopt me?"

The room erupted with laughter. Dr. Johnson clapped his hands again, "Alright folks, let's dig into

Michelle's peach cobbler!"

In a flash, everyone clamored for plates.

• • •

On the back porch, Brandi, Amber, and Nia ate their desserts in silence. "I'm not leaving forever you know..." Her friends nodded with their mouths full. "I keep thinkin' about how weird it's gonna be at Galstanberry without y'all!"

Nia twirled her spoon in the ice cream. "It's good that you're going."

"For real?"

Amber nudged Brandi. "Who else? You're super smart and motivated." She then filled her mouth with ice cream. "You dasurrrve it!"

Brandi squinted her eyes. "Girl, mouth closed! Eat with your mouth closed!" The three laughed. "But, you guys are right. It's probably not gonna be that bad. Plus, we'll have so much to talk about when I come back for Thanksgiving and Christmas."

Nia perked up. "Yeah, and we'll give you a run of all the gossip. She paused, and then smiled slyly, "Do you think Jermaine will still like Tamika?"

Amber scrunched her forehead. "Who won't Jermaine like?! He falls in love with every girl!"

Nia looked from side to side and then leaned in, "Are you gonna miss Joey?"

Brandi rolled her eyes. "Please, girl, I am NOT thinkin' about him?"

"O-Oh, r-realy?" Amber teased as she batted her eyelashes.

"I-I d-don't b-believe you!" Nia chimed in. Brandi hit both of them. "I don't stutter THAT bad around him!"

Her friends burst with laughter, knowing that Brandi was embarrassingly awkward around boys she liked.

"When I get to Galstanberry, I'm going to miss ya'll soo much. For real! We're B.F.F.F.Ls (best friends for fricken life)! No one can come close!"

Dr. Johnson opened the screened door, startling the three friends. "Brandi, come inside and say goodbye to your guests."

• • •

When the last person left, Brandi collapsed on one of the leather couches in the library. "I'm soo tired."

"Good, that means you'll sleep well," Dr. Johnson commented as she plopped beside her daughter. "Remember, we fly early tomo—"

<Beep, Beep>

Her mother checked her pager then looked at the wall clock. "It looks like one of my patient's needs me. I probably won't be back until late tonight. So, make sure everything is packed."

Brandi pulled down one of her curls. "I'll ask Tamara to help me finish some stuff."

"Good. See you bright and early!" She kissed Brandi on the forehead and then grabbed her white coat as she left the house. After taking some grapes from the kitchen, Brandi headed towards her room. She sat on the bed and read the list of school supplies enclosed with the acceptance letter. "Okay, I have folders, my laptop, pencils, and pens. What else?"

"How about my heart necklace?" Tamara asked while it dangled from her fingers in front of Brandi's eyes.

Brandi returned her gaze to the paper. "Nice try. I've learned my lesson. Not to take stuff with—"

"It's yours."

"Really?"

"Look, I CAN take it back…"

"No!" Brandi snatched it from her sister's hands placed it in her jewelry bag. Tamara opened a suitcase and began to look through it. "You sure everything's there?"

"Yeah, all that's listed."

Tamara pointed to a pair of pink ballet shoes. "And how about those?" Brandi smiled and delicately packed them in her bag.

"Alright Dee, it looks like everything's good. So, I'm off to bed. Goodnight, Sis."

"Goodnight."

Brandi changed into her PINK pajamas and snuggled under the covers. She opened her diary and wrote:

> *First, I'll ace Ga-a-lstanberry.*
> *Second, I'll conquer H-a-a-rvard.*
> *And last, the White House!*

San Francisco, California

August 15, 2010

Dear Diary,

The Breakdancing Queen reigns again!! I spun around, kicked my pumas and proved the "D" in my DNA stands for dancing! LOL! Those guys @ the park never saw it coming!

I ran home to tell Mom and Dad, but was held hostage to another lab story. It went something like this: Blah blah, mice, blah blah, chemicals! Really? Is it sooo hard for them to understand that science just isn't my thing?! Before my eyes glazed over, Dad handed me a big envelope from Galstanberry. Seeing the word "acceptance" was like winning my first dance battle—complete euphoria!

Anyway, gotta go and practice footwork for Sunday!

Fiyah in my Feet,
FEI

Fei

Sunday, August 29, 2010

"Look,

if you had... one shot... one opportunity
To seize everything you ever wanted... one moment
Would you capture it? Or just let it slip?"[1]

A figure sat on the asphalt bobbing its head up and down. The big headphones, resembling those worn circa 1990, matched the shiny, red glasses. A microphone screeched, causing everyone to wince in pain. "Yo! Yo! Check one, check two! Hold up, is this even workin'?" The tech by the speakers shrugged. She closed her eyes and bobbed again:

"You better lose yourself in the music, the moment.
You own it, you better never let it go.
You only get one shot, do not miss your chance to blow.
This opportunity comes once in a lifetime, Yo!"[1]

"What if you lose?"

Fei opened her eyes and smiled. "What if I win, Drew?" She loosened her shoelaces and tied them for the

[1] "Loose Yourself," by Eminem

second time—a tradition started at her first competition. She then kissed the index and middle fingers of her right hand and placed them on her left high-top Converse.

Andrew covered his eyes, and shook his head in disapproval. "I don't know why you do that! It's completely unsanitary!"

Must he be so dramatic?

"Live a little, Drew—really!"

"Welcome to the Fourth Annual B-boy Competition. For those who don't know, they beddah?"

"Ask somebody!" The crowd replied excitedly.

"That's right! DJ Kudro here, representin' Hot 97. Today, we compete but also celebrate the art of B-boying. It originated from Hip-Hop and has taken the world by storm. Guys in Moscow are top rockin', while dudes in China perfect the windmill." People nodded proudly as if marching on Washington. "From Brooklyn to Detroit, people are bouncin' to the beat of the streets." Stomps, whistles, and cheers shook the ground like a magnitude seven earthquake on the Richter scale.

"B-boying?" Andrew whispered to Fei.

She looked at him like he was crazy. "It's short for breakdancing. Shh!"

Why, oh, why did I bring him along?

"The first round is elimination—no second chances, no lifelines, no phone a friend. None of that! You'll be judged on creativity, technique and attitude. The fortunate will move to the final round in the evening." He paused to look at the sea of faces, "Some people say B-boying is pointless!"

"Nooo! Boo!!"

DJ Kudrow paced the stage. "I know, I know! Some ask, what's the big deal? And you know what I say?" His arm pointed to the crowd. "THIS is a big deal! Leeeeet's gooooo!"

Although it was nine in the morning on a Sunday, the electricity and the excitement in the air were tremendous. Californians came to watch, while college students hungered to compete.

"This line is long! What's your number?" Andrew peeked at the paper taped to Fei's back, "Fifty!"

She rolled her eyes, "If someone had found their allergy meds sooner, then we could have been here a lot earlier. But whatever, I'm not freakin' out—what's meant to be, will be." Typical Fei, fifty-percent cool and fifty-percent confident. She removed bottled water from a backpack, "Want one?"

"Well, Fei, since I'll probably turn eighty-years-old in this line, I'll save the water until I'm dying of thirst." He huffed and removed a math assignment from his bag.

Sitting on the asphalt, his pencil feverishly wrote, then erased answers. It was a vicious cycle—write a number, erase it, write a number, erase it. After several unsuccessful attempts to solve the problem, he sought help from the master. "Fei, what's the answer to this problem?"

She peered at it, then after two minutes stated, "X equals 21."

"Are you sure? I mean, how'd you get twenty-one, and not fifteen or thirty-two?"

She took his pencil. "Remember the order of operations?" Silence. "Oookay, obviously not. It's P.E.R.M.D.A.S."

"Huh?"

"Drew, do you wear ear plugs in class?"

"Not rea—"

"Never mind! P.E.R.M.D.A.S. It stands for: parentheses, exponents, radicals, multiplication, division, addition, and subtraction."

"What are radicals?"

"They're…You haven't learned that yet."

"Sor-ry, Fei! Not all of us are in super-math like you!" She shrugged, stood up, and sipped her water. Andrew panicked, "Okay, okay! I didn't mean that!"

"Drew, do you want my help or not?" He nodded. "Then, SHHH!! Use PERMDAS to find the right operation to do first. Try the next one."

After a few minutes, he finished the problem. "How's this?"

She gave the nod of approval and stood to scope out her competition. Guys taller and bigger than her walked past. And from what she could see, few girls were present. Suddenly, loud cheers erupted near a hot dog stand. "Drew, save my spot, I'll be back."

"Wait, what?! Where are you...?" His voice faded as she ran towards the bustling group. She squeezed her head between two people. A tall guy wearing a Lakers jersey pointed to himself and shouted from the circle's center, "I'm the baddest B-boy in Cali! That's right, B.A.D is my middle name!"

"Prove it then!" An observer yelled in response.

The guy spun on the ground, back-flipped and then landed in the splits. "Like I said, I'm the baddest!" He shouted while running around the circle of people and slapping their hands.

Fei staggered away holding her stomach. "What's wrong? Are you okay?"

"I-I think so…"

"Sit and tell me what happened. All I could hear was shouting." She sat and closed her eyes.

I can do this! I can do this!

"Fei? Fei?"

She stood, fixed her pig tails, and smiled confidently. "I'm totally cool." His eyes scrutinized her face until she nodded an okay.

"Fei, let's talk about something else. So, you're excited about tomorrow, right?"

"Definitely!"

"What's the n—?"

"Galstanberry Girls Academy."

"So, why'd you apply? The school's on the other side of the country!"

"Mr. Pallzio told me about it. I went to their website and liked basically everything—the classes, extracurriculars. When I told my parents, they said I could only go if I got a scholarship."

"Yeah, schools like that cost about a million anyway."

"I got all the financial aid info together, wrote a really good essay and sent it off!" She smiled thinking of all her hard work.

"I'm proud of you, Fei, seriously."

"Thanks. But now, I have to focus."

She closed her eyes to rehearse the dance combination.

Toprock to get the crowd going. Walk around the stage a couple of times. Then, down to the floor for scissors. Wait, should I do the—

"Numba Fifty!" DJ Kudrow announced. Fei walked slowly onto the stage as if cement blocks were attached to her feet. "Fifty, lets go, you're wastin' time!" She nodded and tucked the green RUN DMC shirt into her purple skinny jeans. A guy in the DJ booth shouted, "Where's ya music?"

"Drew, get it outta my bag!" He walked onto the stage and shyly waved to the judges. The crowd laughed in response.

Great, they'll think I'm a joke!

"Begin when the first beat drops!" When the horn blared from the speakers, it was go time.

Her Converse stomped to the snare of the beat and began footwork. The judges, skeptical at first, began to nod their heads and tap their shoes. "Are you reeeady?" She shouted while lifting her arms up and down.

"What's your friend's name?" A young woman wearing a black-and-white striped shirt and khaki cargo pants asked Andrew.

"Fei, and she practices all the time!"

"Well, her hardwork is DEFINITELY paying off!"

Fei concluded by spinning on the ground with her arms outstretched like a windmill. The judges lifted three score cards into the air.

Really? All 10's! I got all 10's!!

"Thank you! Thank you!" She repeated while shaking the judge's hands. "DJ Kudro, I-I listen to HOT 97 all the time!"

"Thanks. And you are?"

"Fei, but everyone calls me the Breakdancing Queen."

"Everyone?"

"People at school!"

"No doubt you got skills." He looked at a stack of numbered cards. "You're twenty in the finals." She took off her red glasses and rubbed her eyes. "Really?"

"Yeah, why not?" Fei's hands trembled as she removed the card from his hands.

Final round? Really? Me?

"Numba fifty-one, you're up!" As Fei descended the stage steps, Andrew rushed to meet her. "You blew me away!"

Her smile faded when she flipped her phone open. "Ahh! I promised my dad that I'd help him in the lab. And it's probably going to take for-ever!"

"So, whatcha going to do?"

"I'll work for two hours then—" She peered at him slyly.

"And then what, Fei?"

"You'll help my dad out."

He stretched his ear. "Sorry, didn't hear you. What?"

She asked louder, "Can you help my dad out?"

He stepped back. "Laboratories and mice give me the creeps! Those scary red eyes and pink tails…"

She sighed loudly. "Drew, they're babies and don't bite. Pleeease!! I'd do it for you!"

He contemplated her proposal and then answered, "Fine! But remember—"

"Yeah, yeah, yeah. I'll owe you!" They immediately boarded the bus for UCLA.

• • •

Bright lights shone on the immaculately clean laboratory. "Hey, Bàba[2]!"

"Nǐ hǎo[3], Fei!" Dr. Chin greeted in a strong Chinese accent. He stuck a pen in his white coat while studying a specimen through the microscope. "Thank you for coming in."

"Sure! Dad, you remember Andrew, my friend from school."

"Oh yes. Hello, Andrew." He turned around to shake his hand.

"Kě yǐ chī ma[4], Dr. Chin," Andrew recited proudly as Fei shook her head in embarrassment.

Dr. Chin chuckled. "Your friend is apparently hungry."

[2] Dad; [3] Hello; [4] Can we eat?

"No, no, I'm not. In fact, I ate a corn dog at the dance comp—"

"Good call Dad! We'll check the fridge in the conference room." Once inside, she closed the door and slowly walked towards Andrew. "Do not, I repeat, do NOT, mention the B-boy competition."

"Yeah, yeah, I know the drill! But, what's up with your dad asking if I'm hungry?"

"Because, genius, you asked if we could eat!" His cheeks turned bright red. She immediately blocked the doorway. "Don't freak out! You don't need to apologize. But you can talk to him in English. We talk in Chinese because it's comfortable, that's all."

When they re-entered the lab, two white coats were placed on the table. "One day, Fei, you and I will work side by side. You'll get your PhD in Biology and conduct research for your dissertation right here!" Dr. Chin stated proudly as Fei helped Andrew button his lab coat.

"Today, you two will count pups and make a catalog of the total number and specific strain. Mark that information on a sheet of paper and on the cage."

"I can do that, Dr. Chin!" Andrew commented, intent on pleasing him. Two cages were placed side by side; one was empty, while the other contained mice.

Fei placed one of the babies in her hand. "See, not bad. Cute, right?" Andrew ran his finger over the tiny black fur and smiled. "First, we place mom and dad in this clean cage. After each baby is counted we'll put them with their parents." She carefully grabbed one of the adults by its pink tail and placed it in the clean cage. "See, it's not that hard."

He shook his head. "Do it again."

She placed the other parent in the clean cage with ease. Andrew however was not as lucky. Every time he reached for the mouse, it ran to the opposite side of the cage. "Come here! Come here!" Fei pushed him aside.

"Watch me one more time. Wait for the mouse to get calm." Her glove entered the cage. "And then care-ful-ly and quiet-ly grab the tail. Please don't yell, it frightens them. Now, let's count. Hmm, there are one, two, three… eight pups. Can you write that on the cage and that spreadsheet over there? The strain is Er81Cre."

After two hours of work, Andrew cleared his throat. "Fei, we make a good team you know."

Here he goes again.

"We should work together more often. Well, not here anyway."

She rolled her eyes. "Drew, there are six, no, seven pups in this cage. The strain is RosaCre."

He threw down the pen. "Fine, discard my declaration of love!"

Dr. Chin turned around from the microscope at the opposite end of the laboratory. "Is everything alright down there?"

"We're fine, Dad."

When her father exited the lab, Fei turned to Andrew. "Declaration of love? Drew, really?" She covered one of the cages. "You're my best friend. Let's just stay that way, okay?" He nodded although his heart felt like it had been kicked like a soccer ball.

"Almost done?" Her father asked as he re-entered the lab.

"Soon, Dad." At that instant, her phone beeped. She took a furtive glance at her father and whispered, "It's time for me to go back." Andrew looked at the ground. "I'll stay, Fei. And don't worry, you won't owe me. Our friendship is eno—" Before he finished, she slapped his back. "You're the absolute best, Drew!"

"Dad, I have to leave." Dr. Chin looked up from the microscope surprised.

"And go where?"

"Um, well…"

> *Think Fei, think! The longer I wait,*
> *the greater probability he'll—*

"Samantha!" Andrew yelled from across the lab.

She hit her forehead. "Exactly! How could I forget? Mrs. Williams added an extra tutorial session for Samantha. She has a test tomorrow. A very, very hard multiplication test."

"Is that so?" He glanced at the stacks of unmarked cages. "It looks like pups still need to be counted."

"Don't worry. Andrew's gonna finish it for me."

"That's right, Dr. Chin, I'm your man. If there's anything more, then—"

"No, Andrew, counting pups is sufficient, thank you. Fei, make sure to be home before six. Your mother is making your favorite dish." It was obvious that she wasn't telling the complete truth. But, he would address it later.

• • •

Fei raced out of the lab and chased the bus until it finally stopped. The driver chuckled as she placed fare in the change machine, "You must really need to get somewhere!"

"Yeah, I'm a finalist in the B-Boy competition."

"You?"

"Yes, me. In fact, DJ Kudrow said I had skills."

"DJ Kudro, huh? My son Antoine is about your age and listens to him all the time. Can't wait to tell him I've met a celebrity." Fei collapsed in a seat and checked her watch.

Ten minutes! Ten minutes to check in!

As the bus approached downtown, it became increasingly hard to drive through the crowds. "Look, it's gonna take me forever to get through this traffic. Get off here, walk about a block, and take a left."

"Thanks!"

"No problem and good luck!"

Fei maneuvered through the crowds, and, after a few minutes saw the stage in the distance. Her heart pounded as she ran to the check-in table. "Hi, my name's Fei. I'd like to sign in for finals."

A woman with dread locks raised her eyebrows in astonishment. "Excuse me?"

"I should be on the list somewhere."

"Hmm, you look kinda young." She commented while flipping through the roster. Fei peeked over the table, but couldn't see anything. "Fei Chin? Is that you?"

"That's me!"

"Do you have your number?"

Fei dug into her backpack and handed it over. "Yep, I'm twenty."

"Alright, you're officially in. Please excuse my reaction; we're not used to kids, well, your age, making it this far. So, big congrats!"

"Thanks."

"Stay around the stage. In about fifteen minutes DJ Kudrow will make announcements."

"Great! See ya later!" Fei sat at a nearby bench and watched the bustling activity.

If Mom and Dad could see all these people they'd flip!

The microphone screeched as DJ. Kudrow maneuvered it. "Are you ready for the biggest, and baddest final round?"

"Yeahhhh!"

"As you know, I'm DJ Kudro representin' HOT 97, and this is the finals. The Grand Prize is five-hundred dollas and an opportunity to tour with QueenBeats." The crowd cheered as five women stepped onto the stage.

"QueenBeats have been on MTV's *America's Best Dance Crew* and featured in numerous commercials. Second place is three-hundred dollas, and third, two-hundred dollas. Alright, I'm ready, are y'all?"

"Yeaah!"

"Naw, y'all ain't ready. I said, 'are y'all READY?!'"

"Yeeeeahhhhh!!!!"

"There will be twenty competitors, with six-minute sets."

Twenty! What?! I'm last!

Fei walked backstage and approached a woman holding a clipboard and wearing a head set. "Where should I go?"

"What's your number, hun?"

"Twenty."

"Good, you're easy. The line is over there, just go to the end." A tall lanky guy wearing a white t-shirt and faded black jeans turned around. "Last, huh?"

"Yep."

"You look young. How old ar—"

"Twelve."

"Twelve-years-old! For real? Shouldn't you be playing with dolls or something?"

"What?!"

"Yeah, painting your nails?"

She rolled her eyes. "Really, painting my nails? That's a little harsh." She searched her backpack for her dance music.

"So, uh, where are your parents?" He looked around for an Asian couple waiting for their daughter. Even though the CD was now in her hands, she continued to fake looking for it.

"They, um, couldn't make it."

"Well, whatever. I give you mad props for having the courage to compete. So, good luck, man; I mean, girl." He turned around and bobbed his head to the music in his iPod.

As the hour progressed, Fei moved closer to the stage. She couldn't see the performances but could hear the crowd's reactions.

What will they think of me?

"Numba nineteen!"

The lanky guy turned to Fei with eyes filled with excitement. "I'm up, good luck!" When the music began, his feet engaged in a complicated footwork sequence. He then slid across the stage on his stomach.

"Fei! Fei!" She turned around to a sweating and out-of-breath Andrew. "I-I wanted to g-get here before you got on stage!"

"Really?!"

"Yeah, I don't want you to worry."

"I'm not! In fact, I'll leave them speech-less!"

"Numba twenty!" She squeezed his hand, walked onto the stage, and handed her music to the DJ.

Definitely more people than this morning...

The music started, but she stood and stared at the crowd. Her mind was racing.

> *Soo many people. Too many people.*
> *Soo many people. Too many people...*

"Alright, numba twenty, one more time." Once again the music started, but still no movement.

"Breakdancing Queen!" Andrew yelled. She shook her head then turned to DJ Kudro and the panel of judges. "I-I'm ready. Just give me one more shot."

As soon as the music blared through the speakers, Fei walked to the stage's edge and threw her hands in the air to hype the crowd. After running in swift circles, she froze in the center of the stage for thirty seconds. Her left hand was under her chin and her right arm rested on her hip.

One, two, three!

She hit the ground and spun with her knees hugged to her chest. Then she jumped up, moonwalked to the right of the stage, back-flipped to the center, and stood with arms folded. A roar of cheers followed as she descended the stairs backstage.

I-I did it!

DJ Kudrow returned to the stage. "Big props to all the competitors today! The judges will tally the results in a few minutes."

"Do you think I placed?"

Andrew shrugged. "C'mon, does it really matter?"

"Of course it does! Hello? I didn't prepare for months to lose! I am NOT a loser!"

He tapped his foot nervously. "Well, the results better be announced soon because you need to be home by six."

The crowd grew silent as DJ Kudrow reappeared with

three envelopes. "In third place for two-hundred dollas is numba five, Jamal Simmons. Second place, for three-hundred dollas is numba sixteen, Matthew Williams." Fei and Andrew both gripped each other for dear life. "I think you won."

DJ Kudrow cleared his throat. "And the Grand Prize of five-hundred dollas, and the opportunity to tour with QueenBeats is…" As he slowly opened the envelope, Fei squeezed her eyes tight.

Please, pleeeeease!

"Numba nineteen, Anthony Johnson!" The lanky guy leaped onto the stage and slapped DJ Kudrow's hand. Fei's heart sank to the ground. It was like someone had stolen her yellow, high–top Keds.

"Fei, it was a long shot anyway, right?"

Don't cry, you're too strong to cry.

"I'm fine, not sweating it." But every bone in her body ached. As the two somberly walked away from the stage, a woman ran behind them.

"Hey! Wait!" Fei didn't break her stride; she was too distraught to speak. When Andrew turned around, the woman asked, "Where's your friend going?"

"Fei! Wait a minute!"

"Come on, Drew!"

"Fei, I'm serious. Stop walking!!"

"What?!" She whipped around with her pig tails flying behind.

Is that..?

A slow smile formed as she approached the woman and Andrew. "You're one of the *QueenBeats!*" Her hand shot out. "I'm Fei, Fei Chin!"

"It's Breakdancin' Queen!" Andrew corrected.

She pushed him aside. "Or just Fei, or whatever..."

"I'm Lady—"

"Gemz! You're on MTV all the time!!"

"Good. So, you can let go of my hand now."

"Oh, sorry!"

"No worries. You held your own up there." Suddenly, Fei remembered her loss.

"Doesn't matter. I—"

"Yes, you lost. What's the plan now?" Fei kicked a rock on the ground.

Curl up in a ball and disappear into oblivion!

"Look, Queen, I'll tell you what you're NOT going to do."

Fei rolled her eyes. "And that is?"

Lady Gemz stepped closer. "Give up! You have

incredible talent!"

"Talent? Yeah, right..."

"We have a summer camp just for B-girls like you."

A grin broke out on Fei's face before she wrapped her arms around Lady Gemz's waist. "Thank you! Thank you!"

"Just get your parent's permission and you're set to go!"

Fei quickly drew back. "Parent's permission?"

Lady Gemz winced as her ringtone went off. "Sorry, I gotta go. But, here's my business card. Look forward to seeing you this summer, Fei!"

"It's Breakdancin' Queen!" She shouted with renewed confidence. Andrew and Fei resumed their walk to the bus stop. "I can spend the whole summer dancing! Incredible, right Drew?"

He frowned. "I know you're happy right now. But we're fifteen minutes late!" They immediately sprinted to the bus stop.

• • •

On Fei's porch, Andrew rocked back and forth on his heels. "Soooo, guess this is it, huh?"

She looked away and replied with a tinge of sadness, "Don't worry, I'll email and stuff." The screen door squeaked as it opened. "Fei, is that you?"

"Yes, Dad."

"You are late!" Andrew cleared his throat.

"Oh, hello again, Andrew."

"Hi, Dr. Chin. Again, it was a pleasure working with you today. Frankly, it's my fault Fei's late tonight. I should have paid more att—"

"Nonsense, Fei should have been more responsible. You two have less than ten minutes to say goodbye." When he left, she gave Andrew an apologetic look. "Thanks. But, you didn't have to."

He ran a hand through his dirty-blonde hair. "Anything for you, Fei. I'm gonna really miss you—as a friend, of course." After a couple of seconds, Andrew gave her another hug. "See ya, Fei!"

"See ya, Andrew!"

She walked into the house and locked the door.

"Wait! Wait!"

Fei leaned her ear toward the door, "Yeah?"

"I have, um, a card for you. Open it when you get there, okay?" He slipped it under the door and only left when she picked it up.

A card?

"Feeeeei!!!"

Great, and now on to the firing squad.

"Where were you?" Mrs. Chin sternly questioned as Fei cautiously entered the dining room.

"I was tutoring Samantha, Dad knows."

Dr. Chin slowly approached her. "We are going to ask you one last time. Where were you Fei Chin?"

She sat down at the dining table. "I was at a dance competition."

He removed a crumpled flyer from his pocket.

Darn! I forgot to throw that away!

"This break competition?"

"Its break dancing," She mumbled under her breath.

"Fei, you don't need to lie to your mother and I."

"But you wouldn't have let me go!"

Mrs. Chin put a tea pot on the stove. "How do you know? You didn't even give us a chance."

Now, Fei was annoyed. Why would they suddenly change their minds? She sat up straight with a surge of indignation. "Give you a chance? Really?! Since when did you EVER give my dancing a chance?"

Dr. Chin shook his head. "It's a hobby, Fei, that is all. You can not make a career out of it!"

Mrs. Chin turned off the squealing teapot. "Your father's right. Science is more stable. And you are good in it."

Fei defiantly crossed her arms. "Just because I'm good, doesn't mean I should do it until I'm a hundred! I hate working with mice. I hate going to the lab!"

Dr. Chin's forehead wrinkled in disapproval. "Science isn't all about mice."

"Well, dancing isn't all about fun. It's hard work, too." She rose from her chair and stood next to his. "Sometimes, I feel like the mice, confined to yours and mom's expectations."

Mrs. Chin shook her head while pouring tea into her husband's tea cup. "Galstanberry will be good for you. You'll forget about that break stuff. Academics will be the focus."

"But—!"

Dr. Chin pounded his fist on the table. "End-of-discussion!" He then cleared his throat and spoke calmly, "Now, I'm sure you are hungry."

Her stomach let out a small growl.

Stop that! Traitor!

"Your mother made your favorite dishes."

"May I be excused?" There was no way she could eat under their stares. Mrs. Chin's face dropped with sadness. "But Fei, I prepared this food."

"May I be excused?" She repeated with greater strength.

Dr. Chin slowly nodded. "Remember, we have a

long plane ride in the morning. Make sure you pack and then go straight to sleep."

• • •

She flicked the light switch and jumped onto the bed. "I'm sooo hungry! I could eat the wall paper!" She pulled Lady Gemz's business card from her back pocket and held it in the air. "Parent's permission, yeah right! They'd never, ever let me go!" She then slid off her bed, opened the closet, and sat inside it. On one of the shelves was a gray boombox. When she reached up to press play, "Walk This Way" remixed by Run-D.M.C. blasted through the speakers.

Her head tilted up to look at the large stacks of shoe boxes. Each were labeled: C, P or F. The 'C' stood for competition, 'P' was for practice, and 'F' meant for fun. "Okay, I'll start from the bottom and work to the top."

She removed the top of each box, and pulled out each different pair. "Definitely my black Pumas, pink Nike Prescos." She held up a black-and-white pair. "And, of course, my old-school Converse."

A knock on the door startled her. "Fei, can I come in?"

"Hold on, Dad! Hoooold on!" She stuffed the shoes in the suitcase and threw Lady Gemz's card in her backpack. "Okay, come in!"

Dr. Chin cautiously entered while holding a brown box. "Fei, can you?"

"Oh, sorry!" She rushed to turn the volume dial down.

"Thank you. I wanted to tell you that despite what happened tonight, your mother and I are very proud of you. You do everything we ask—get good grades, work at the lab." He paused to scratched his head and think of the appropriate words. "Fei, one day you will understand why we push you towards science. We want you to have a good career and be successful."

"Dad, I'm sorry for—"

He held up a hand to stop her. "Your mother saw these and thought you'd like them." She flipped open the top, removed the tissue paper and then rubbed her eyes in shock.

"What?! The new, pink Pumas with Velcro straps!!! Really?!"

But then she remembered her parents' true feelings about her dancing. If she danced in these shoes, they would never come to see. Reluctantly, Fei placed the shoes back and pushed the box over. "I can't take them. You and mom want me to be a scie—"

"Happy, Fei. We want you to be happy. And you'll make the right decision when the time comes."

Huh? What does that mean?

Although she didn't believe the issue was resolved, her parents did acknowledge her passion for dancing.

Baby steps. At least they took baby steps.

She smiled and gave him a hug. "Xie Xie[5]!"

"Okay, I will let you finish packing." As soon as he closed her door, she immediately texted Andrew.

> **FEI:** got new pumas!
> **DREW:** kool!
> **FEI:** think M&D get it now…
> **DREW:** finally! got 2 go
> **FEI:** C ya!

"Okay, pencils, spiral notebooks, sweatshirts. Anything else?" She tossed Andrew's card back and forth. "I won-der what-it-says…"

Before the temptation to rip it open overcame her, she immediately zipped it in the suitcase front pocket. "Out of sight, out of mind!" She put on her Aeropostale pajamas, snuggled under the silk, black comforter, and wrote in her diary.

The Breakdancing Queen reigns again!

[5] Thank you. Pronounced, "Sheh, Sheh!"

Austin, Texas

August 12, 2010

Dear Diary,

Today, Duchess and I leaped! We'll beat Vicki Burnett! She tries to be the best rider of all time! Can we say, 3 B's please? Borrowed horse, Blah clothes, and Bad blonde highlights!!

Crossing fingers that mother can squeeze me in between father's campaign stuff. Geez, I'm just their ONLY child!

What-ev! Each race, play and birthday missed, is a Prada bag, Juicy dress, and cowboy boots gained. Oops, I almost forgot! The Galstanberry envelope came. Of course, I got in. Duh! The REAL question is— do I pack my Gucci dress in the Louis suitcase, or is that trés tacky?

I'm ready for Galstanberry, but highly doubt it can handle me!

> *Fashionably Fabulous,*
> *TABS*

Tabitha

Sunday, August 29, 2010

"Su-ppo-zedly, she got in because Mommy Dearest's a Kappa..." Jayne played with her Tiffany heart charm to avoid Savannah's eyes. It was 'social faux pas' to spread rumors, especially when it pertained to friends. While gazing at the horse stables, she defiantly crossed her arms and continued, "It doesn't hurt that Mr. Crawford's a Gove-nah. I have great grades, too, you know. But obviously, not great enough! Ugh, I don't get it! Luck, like, runs through her blood!"

Savannah puckered her lips in her compact mirror and listened only half-heartedly to her friend's complain-fest, "Rosy Red would've totally been a beddah gloss."

The most affluent families in Austin, Texas filled the seats of the arena for the highly anticipated <u>Heischman Brothers Youth & Adult Equestrian Competition</u>. Each parent hoped that the hundreds of dollars spent on private riding lessons would result in a trophy and consequently bragging rights at tea.

Mothers, aunts and grandmothers donned exquisite hats trimmed specifically for this occasion. Men wore collared shirts with cowboy hats and polo suit jackets.

The horse track's speakers screeched as the announcer moved his microphone. "Our last compe-ti-tah, wearin' numbah twenny-fahv, is Tabitha Crawford, daugh-tah of Gove-nah William Crawford and Mrs. Sandy Kay Crawford." A hush fell over the stadium. The Crawford's legacy of prestige and wealth was widely known throughout Texas. Tabitha mounted the horse by gripping the reigns with her Mark Todd gloves and placing her left Tuffa riding boot into the stirrup. Holding the withers, she pushed up and swung the right leg over the back of the horse.

I will sooo win this race!

"Ladies, at th'a sound of the gun, go!"

At the first shot, horses ran as whistles and shouts filled the air. "Dahhlin', our Tabitha's leadin'!" Mrs. Crawford exclaimed as she looked through pink binoculars. Governor Crawford gave his bottle of Perrier to the waiter, and picked up the matching blue set. "Goshdawg! She is, Sandy!" At the quarter pole, Tabitha and Vicki's horses were neck and neck.

C'mon Duchess, we're almost there!

"Go, Tabitha! Goooo!" Savannah and Jayne screamed at the top of their lungs. Jayne took a sip of lemonade to lubricate her throat. "I think she's gonna beat Vicki this time." Savannah earnestly nodded and put her crossed fingers in the air.

"Folks, it's a close race between numbahs fo-teen and twenny-fahv." Everyone sat at the edge of their seats. As the girls approached the finish line, Vicki's horse inched to the front. "That's it, ladies and gents! It's all ovah! We have numbahs fo-teen in first, twenny-fahv in secon' and thirdy-two in third! Please take yo' horses in an' return ta th'a arena."

Tabitha and Duchess solemnly trotted to the stables. Once in the stall, she wiped tears away with a Burberry handkerchief. "Are you okay, Tabitha?" Vicki asked nervously.

Geez! Why is she talkin' to me?

Tabitha didn't respond with the hope that Vicki would leave. Unfortunately, it only encouraged her to probe further, "Tabitha, you're not hurt, right?"

"No, no, I'm not." But that wasn't the truth. Her second defeat to Vicki was unbearable.

"I-I just wanted to say great race." Tabitha rolled her eyes in annoyance. "You really don't have to." Vicki shrugged and called out, "I'm just tryin' to be nice," as she left the stables.

"I'm just tryin' to be nice!" Tabitha mocked in a high pitch voice while applying pink plush lip gloss. In spite of the loss, a grand entrance was still required. She walked into the arena waving like a newly-crowned Miss America. "Thanks, everybody. Really, you're too kind." She dramatically placed a hand over her heart and faked tears of joy.

"Numbah twenny-fahv, please take yah place i-mmediately."

The crowd chuckled, while Mrs. Crawford swelled with pride. "A stah, William! Our daughtah's a stah!" Tabitha's perpetual confidence made her the leader of the popular group at Cranbrook Academy. Her inner circle included Savannah Pickett, daughter of Dr. Howard Pickett, one of the most sought after plastic surgeons in Texas; and Jayne Mansfield, daughter of Joshua Mansfield, CEO of Heischman Investment Firm. The girls were ecstatic to continue their reign into middle school However, Tabitha's recent Galstanberry acceptance changed everything. What would their lives be like now?

The equestrian winners stood on a three-tiered rostrum as their parents moved to the front row with cameras ready. "Dahhlin', Dahhlin', ovah hea!" Mrs. Crawford waved a handkerchief to get her daughter's attention. "Will-iaaam, I don't think she can hea me!"

He nodded. "Tabitha, sweetheart, ovah hea! Ovah hea!!"

They're so embarrassin'!
I wish I was adopted, better yet, Orphan Annie!

Fortunately, the announcer's voice drowned out her parents antics, "Thank yah ladies for a grand race! Now, fou the trophy pre-sen-tayshun. In third place, Kristin Jopplin; secon' place, Tabitha Crawford; and the grand winnah fou the secon' consecutive yea, Vicki Burnett." Each girl, except Tabitha, beamed from ear to ear for photographs.

"Daahlin', smile! Show those pearly whites! Frowns cause wrrin-kles!" She turned once again to her husband. "Will-iaaam, why isn't she smilin'?" He shrugged and checked his pocket watch. After pictures, Mrs. Crawford's tall, slender frame rushed to embrace Tabitha. "Oh, daahlin', you look lahhvely!"

But Tabitha wiggled out of her embrace. "Mo-thaahh, who cares what I look like?" And then stomped her Tuffas against the dirt. "I lost a-gain!" Governor Crawford took a sip of his Perrier and shook his pudgy finger. "I won't tolerate a hissy fit! You can't win every time."

She shrugged— "can't" was not in her vocabulary. "Do you know how many times I ran for office and lost?!"

Tabitha sighed out loud. "I've heard this a billion times! Three! You lost three times!"

"Exactly! But nevah gave up." He paused, and wiped the sweat that dripped from his chubby, and almost sunburned, face. "Sandy, I can't keep lecturin' her. It's hottah than a goat's behind in a peppah patch!"

Mrs. Crawford gave him another handkerchief and turned to Tabitha. "Your fa-thah and I will have tea with Judge Williams an' his wife. Please return home by fou, no later than fou-thirty, to get dressed for the fundraiser."

"Ugh! Do I havta go? My cheeks get sore from smilin' all the time. And my hands cramp from hand shakin.'"

"Don't be silly, Tabitha! Now, William, if we're late, we'll miss my favorite blueberry scones." They kissed their daughter goodbye and walked towards Starlight Circle.

• • •

Tabitha walked alone and smiled as she passed the horse stables, track and practice grounds. Meanwhile, Savannah and Jayne tiptoed behind her. Suddenly, they shouted, "Boo!!"

She whipped around and was presented with a bouquet of lilies, "Aww, my fave!" The girls began to walk towards the Crystal Garden. "Get this, I'm being forced to attend another black tie!"

"Oh, your life's sooo horrible!" Jayne teased as she playfully hit Tabitha.

"How's the fashionably fabulous Tabs goin' to wow the crowd?" Savannah asked dramatically.

Tabitha unsnapped her black velvet helmet and twirled it on the right finger. Her red hair fell against the dark violet Caldene blazer. "I tol' Sophia to set out a couple a' dresses. It's soo hard to pick an outfit when yah hair's the color of a fire engine." Like Superman feared kryptonite, Tabitha dreaded her red hair. Of course, Mr. Flannel, their science teacher taught about the unpredictability of genes. However, the information didn't console her when she stuck out in family pictures.

"When you become a world famous actress, you'll party with other gorgeous red heads," Jayne stated proudly.

"Like who?!"

"Let's see... Nicole Kidman, Bree from um, that housewives show."

"*Desperate Housewives*," Savannah happily added.

"Yep! Annd Kate Winslet! She not only shares your fab name but was kissed by Leonardo DiCaprio." Suddenly, a high-pitch voice interrupted their pow-wow. "Hey, guys! Are you goin' tah afternoon tea?"

Savannah looked her up and down. "O.M.G! You're still carryin' that thing?"

"Oh, my fosters went to get the car. I'm holdin' my

trophy until they get back."

"Fosters? Like foster parents?"

"Yep!"

Tabitha discretely looked from side to side. A conversation with a known dork like Vicki Burnett could tarnish her perfect image. "Look, we have plans."

As the three continued to walk, Vicki jumped in their paths. "Wait! Don't go! You guys are so popular and stylish. And I just thought—"

"Clearly, you didn't think," Savannah remarked slyly while folding her arms. "And besides, we don't hang out with Salvation Army shoppers anyway." Vicki blushed in embarrassment, while Tabitha looked at her Tuffas. She knew Savannah had crossed the line. But instead of speaking up, she changed the subject, "Sorry, our table's full anyway."

"Of course it is! Who wouldn't want to sit with you guys?"

At that moment, a tall woman wearing a denim dress approached. "Vicki, honey, your dad and I have been callin' you nonstop! Why haven't you picked up the phone?"

"Sorry, Mom, I've been talkin' to my friends."

"Friends?" Savannah whispered in shock.

Tabitha nudged her and stepped forward. "I'm Tabitha Crawford."

Vicki's mother shook her hand. "Really? Gove-nah Crawford's daughtah?"

"Yes, and this is Savannah Pickett and Jayne Mansfield." Each girl smiled weakly.

"It's nice that Vicki will have friends this fall."

"Fall?" Jayne asked in disbelief.

"That's right! She earned a full academic scholarship to attend Cranbrook Middle School."

"Scholarship?" Savannah repeated.

Tabitha grabbed her friend's arms. "Mrs. Burnett, we really have to go. Nice to meet you, bye!"

• • •

The three girls rushed into the Crystal Garden and approached the host podium. He looked up and frowned. "Welcome to the Crystal Garden's Junior Equestrian Tea. If you don't have reservations, don't bother wait'in." Tabitha cleared her throat and in the most dignified voice stated, "Yes, we do. Crawford party, three fou tea."

He shook his head in amazement, "Of course, of course, step this way, Mademoiselles!" All eyes watched the girls strut towards their table like models in Marc Jacob's Spring runway show. "Here are the tea menus. Your server will be here momentarily. Miss Crawford, is there anything else I can do for you?" Like Miranda Priestly would have in *The Devil Wears Prada*, she promptly shooed him away, "That's all!" He bowed and left immediately.

"Tabs, we're treated like rock stars with you!" Jayne gushed as she unraveled the folded napkin, "People like Vicki Burnett don't deserve to be around us stars. I mean seriously, what was she thinking?"

Savannah nodded in agreement. "You're SO right! We were only saving her from complete humiliation! Can you IMAGINE if she hung out with us?"

"That would NEVER happen!"

Savannah rolled her eyes, "Well, duh, Jayne!" She paused to apply her second coat of lip gloss, "Anyway, Vicki couldn't handle our shoppin' trips! Gosh, it makes me sad just thinkin' 'bout it."

Jayne wiped away a fake tear and turned to Tabitha, "Don't yah think so?" She shifted uneasily and looked down at her menu, "Rose Petal or Earl Grey? I can't decide!" The girls chatted about tea possibilities until the server appeared.

"Welcome, ladies, to the Crystal Garden. My name is Frederick and I am your server today. First, we will start with your choice of tea." As usual Tabitha took the lead, "Rose Petal please."

"Good choice. Customers enjoy the bitter, yet sweet taste."

Savannah followed, "I'll take that, too." Jayne rolled

her eyes. "Such-a-follower."

"I'm not!"

"Suuure. An-y-way, I'll take Chamomile Tea." The waiter left to gather the appropriate dishes.

"Frederick's such-a-hottie!" Jayne swooned as she watched him walk away. "So girls, what do we give him?" She and Savannah held up eight fingers, while Tabitha held only four. "Someone's picky." Jayne teased while spreading raspberry jam on a cinnamon scone.

Tabitha straightened her posture, "It's called pre-fer-ence. I prefer tall guys with muscles."

"Muscles, ew!" Savannah squealed like broccoli had been shoved in her face.

"Hello? I just need someone to carry my shoppin' bags!"

The girls laughed until Frederick returned with a gold platter, "We have delectable cucumber tea sandwiches to the left and delicious spring radish to the right. I will return with your tea selections."

Savannah began to stack sandwiches on a plate until Tabitha grabbed her arm. "Stop!! You're embarrassin' us!" She surveyed the scene for witnesses. "You'll be Duchess' size if you keep eatin' like that. Just, watch me." Tabitha cut her sandwich in half and nibbled on a corner. "See, small bites."

"But, I'm soo hungry."

Jayne nudged her arm. "Savannah, you're ALWAYS hungry."

Frederick poured their teas into three purple tea cups. "Are the sandwiches to your liking? I see not many have been eaten." Tabitha batted her eyelashes, "We're fine."

"If you need—"

"Nope!"

"Oookay, dessert in ten, enjoy!"

The girls gently sipped with pinkie fingers in the air.

"Yuck!" Tabitha shouted.

"Awful!" Savannah shrieked.

Jayne dumped sugar cubes into their tea cups.

"Trust me, this helps."

"How can our moms drink this stuff?" Savannah asked as she stuffed a scone into her mouth to eliminate the bitter taste.

"Maybe it gets beddah the oldah you get," Jayne guessed. Tabitha raised her eyebrows, "Oldah? Wrinkles are totally scared of my ma-thah's face. Sometimes, it looks like a frozen popsicle, kinda like this!" She pulled her face back so much that her eyes appeared like little slits. The girls burst with laughter.

"Tabs, wh-what will we do with-without you?" Savannah asked through breaths of laughter. Jayne wiped her tears away. "School's goin' to be so blah-ze!"

"I'm not moving to Antarctica! We can text and IM 24/7."

And what about school, Miss Crawford?" Jayne teased in a mother-like tone.

"School, shmool. I can't wait to par-tay! Which reminds me..." She gently tapped her water glass with a fork, "I'd like to make a toast!" The girls raised their glasses. "To me ruling Galstanberry, and fantabulous friends!" They clinked glasses and delicately sipped lemon water.

Jayne however was still a little envious of her friend's acceptance. "Tabs, you know I'm really happy for you right?" Tabitha nodded. "But, don't you think it's a little weird that you got in and we didn't?" Savannah kicked her under the table. "Think about it, we all have the same grades and volunteer hours."

"Stop it, Jayne!" Savannah warned.

"Or what? You'll eat yourself 'til you explode!"

Tabitha narrowed her eyes, "Why not me?! Are you sayin' I don't de-serve to be a Galstanberry girl?" Jayne popped a grape into her mouth, "Let's just say daddy being a Gove-nah definitely helped." Tabitha looked at Savannah, who immediately looked away. Jayne nodded, "Oh, Savannah thinks so, too. She's just too chicken to say it."

"What?! You guys talk about me behind my back!" The girls were silent.

Fine, if they want to be mean, I can be mean, too!

"Jayne, you are soo predictable. You've always been jealous of me." Her eyebrows rose in response. "Don't look surprised! The Gove-nah's mansion is way bigger than yours. And Savannah, you've always wanted to be skinny like me. It's not my fault your fatness is…is repulsive!"

Savannah's eyes began to fill with tears. "Tabitha, you know I've been tryin' to lose weight." The waiter returned with chocolate truffles. "Straight from the oven ladies!" Tabitha took a bite and then smiled slyly. "Mmm, good. But, Frederick, be a dear, and take some away. We don't want to get fat like SOME people."

Savannah stared at the tablecloth completely humiliated. Jayne turned to the bewildered waiter, "Could you give us a sec?" Sensing the tension, he left immediately. "Look Miss Gove-nah's daughtah, Miss Perfect, Miss Whatevah-you-want-people-to-call-you. There's no need to go Cruella de Vil on us!" Tabitha ignored her, "It's good that I'm leavin' for Galstanberry tomorrow. I was gettin' tired of you guys anyway." She took two more sips of her tea and left.

• • •

At the front door of the country club, tears streamed down Tabitha's cheeks as she texted her driver.

Ugh! My mascara's not waterproof!!

A black Mercedes with tinted windows approached. Charlie, her chauffeur, opened the back passenger door and offered her a red cashmere pashmina. He noticed that it matched the tint of her eyes. "Hello, Miss Crawford. How was the race today?" Like a Hollywood diva eluding the press, she delicately put on a pair of oversized CHANEL sunglasses, threw the pashmina over her right shoulder, and concisely answered, "Fine, please take me home." Usually the car was filled with lively discussion, but today only silence. "Miss, if you want to talk about it..." No answer. "There is tissue in the front pocket." After ten minutes, she finally spoke, "I don't have any friends."

"Nonsense, Miss Crawford! Every girl at Cranbrook wants to befriend you."

"That's totally the problem! I'm picked first for teams, my lunch table's always full, and when I wea Hardcandy, guess what happens." He shrugged. "The girls wea it the next day!" She huffed and folded her hands. "Ugh, nevah mind! You don't even have kids!"

He turned down the air conditioning, "Miss Crawford, I actually have three daughters."

She sat up straight and lifted one eyebrow. "Three? Why didn't you tell me?"

He shifted uncomfortably. "You never asked."

Am I seriously that awful?

"But, Miss Crawford, I enjoy talkin' 'bout your life and friends."

My life, my friends. Ugh! I AM totally awful!!!!

The guilt she felt when Savannah teased Vicki crept up again.

Not this time! I can totally fix this!

"What are their names? How old are they?"

A smile spread on his face. "Well, Kelly just turned sixteen."

"Was her sweet sixteen fab?! What about her dress?"

"It was—"

"Wait! Don't tell me! Betsey Johnson-fun or Saks-classic?"

"My wife made a special dress and the party was small, but nice."

Great. Tabitha-0,
Charlie (a.k.a. Mother Teresa's twin brother)-2.

"Well, um, how about the other girls?"

The iron gates opened when Charlie tipped his hat to the guardsmen, "Amanda is eleven an—"

"Same age as me!"

He continued, "And my youngest, Melissa, is five". She leaned on the divider that separated driver from passenger, "I'd like to meet Mandy."

"Miss Crawford, it's Amanda."

"I know, but she'd love Mandy more. We could ride horses and have tea!"

Sophia, the head maid, opened the limousine's door. "Good afternoon, Miss Crawford!"

Tabitha gave her the red pashmina, "Sophia, did you know Charlie has three girls? One's even my age."

Yes, Amanda's a delightful girl."

"What? Why was I the last to know?"

As her Tuffa's angrily stomped up the marble stairs, Sophia yelled, "Don't forget to—"

"I know, I know!" Before entering the room, she unzipped her boots and placed them outside the door to be cleaned.

• • •

The sun's rays illuminated her crystal chandelier and made her lavish bedroom room sparkle. She moved the sapphire, emerald and canary-yellow dresses to the right side of the bed and placed her head on the plum pillows. "Miss Crawford, have you showered?"

"Sophia, I'm too stressed to go!"

She stood above Tabitha with her arms folded, "No, you're not! Now try on those dresses!"

Tabitha pounded her fist into the comforter, "No! I won't." Then, after returning her head to the pillow she said, "Plus, you're not Mrs. Sandy Kay Crawford!"

Sophia picked up the phone, "Shall I call her then?" Tabitha jumped up and rushed into the bathroom. After a long hot shower, she tied the magenta bath robe around her waist. Sophia reappeared with a silver platter.

"Is there whip cream?"

"Miss Crawford, it is the same strawberry shake I've made for years. Now, what dress have you selected?" Tabitha shrugged. "Fine, you may have a few minutes to think." Tabitha dipped the cherry into her mouth and then dug into the whip cream. While sipping through the straw, she examined her face in the vanity mirror. "Stupid freckles, why am I the only Crawford cursed with them?" Suddenly, her hot pink phone rung.

Who could that be?

"Hello, Tabitha Crawford."

She twirled the cord around her finger. "Miss Crawford, your ma-thah just called."

"Riiight…"

"And she strongly encourages you to wea the

emerald dress."

"Why?"

"It will en-hance yah eyes."

And bring out my stupid freckles…" Tabitha quietly mumbled.

"What was that, Miss Crawford?"

"I said, is that it, Sophia?"

"Yes."

She hung up the phone and held the emerald dress in the air. "En-hance my eyes, yeah right." She then grabbed the sapphire dress and rushed behind her bamboo folding screen. When she tried to pull the zipper up, it wouldn't budge. "Ugh, Sooo-phiii-a!!!" Tabitha stepped from behind the screen. "You picked a dress that's too small!"

Sophia wrinkled her forehead and tried to pull the zipper up, "Miss Crawford, it can't be small! You purchased this a few weeks ago!" Finally the zipper moved, "It is up!"

Tabitha held in her stomach as she modeled the dress. "Miss Crawford, stop that! You're turnin' red like a ripe tomato!"

"Sophia!! I-I can't breathe!! I'm goin' to die!!!" After Sophia hastily pulled the zipper, Tabitha collapsed on the bed. "Shall I get the doctor, Miss Crawford?" Tabitha rolled her eyes and changed into the canary-colored dress.

"Ooo, much beddah!" She rushed to the mirror. "It's cute, right, Sophia?"

"It will do."

"That's NOT the answer I was lookin' fou. Does it say Gove-nah's daughtah?"

Sophia held the emerald dress. "Try your ma-thah's suggestion."

Tabitha draped it over her arm and disappeared once more. When she emerged, she cautiously walked towards the mirror. "It's per-fect!"

"Yes it is Miss Crawford. Now, how 'bout jewelry?" Tabitha opened a burgundy velvet box and removed a pearl necklace. After it was secured around her neck, she slipped on a pair of black sequined ballet flats and fluffed out her hair.

As Tabitha walked toward the door, Sophia placed a Croc lime clutch in her hands and shooed her downstairs, "Your parents are wait'in at Constitution Hall."

"What? We're not goin' togethah?"

Sophia sighed and opened the limousine door, "Miss Crawford, must we go ovah this again?" Tabitha shook her head and slid across the leather backseat.

• • •

As the limo pulled out of the gates, her clutch vibrated, "I swear if Savannah and Jayne—" She flipped open the phone and yelled, "What?!"

"Excuse me, young lady?" Mrs. Crawford asked in

an irritated voice. "I'm sorry, I just th—"

"Tabitha Marie Crawford. Don't EVAH use that tone with me! I'm your ma-thah, not the gardenah!"

"Yes, ma'am."

"Well anyway, people are lookin' forward to seein' you!"

Sure they are.

"And, guess who's here?"

"Who?" She asked with fake interest.

"The Picketts with Savannah! I'm so glad you girls are friends." Tabitha rolled her eyes and brought the phone away from her mouth, "I have a bad con-nec-shun."

"What, daahlin'?"

"Can-not hea you!" Mrs. Crawford spoke louder, "Your fa-thah is approachin' the microphone. Au revoir!" Tabitha snapped the phone shut then folded her arms.

Once the limo halted, and Tabitha's flats hit the red carpet, blubs flashed from all directions. "Miss Crawford! Miss Crawford! Look hea!" She smiled and posed with her hands on her hips. "To yah left, Miss Crawford! No, this-a-way!" When her clutch vibrated, she waved and raced into the building.

A young man wearing a pinstriped suit rushed towards her. "You're late!" He took her hand and led her down a long hallway.

"It's nice to see you too, Sam," she responded sarcastically.

"I promised to deliver you to your parents."

"What? I'm like mail now?!" They turned a corner and entered the ballroom. Mrs. Crawford immediately stood up as they approached, "Thank you for escortin' her Samuel." He smiled and hurried backstage. "Savannah came by lookin' for you. Did you two get to see each other?" Tabitha sat down and sipped a glass of water. "No."

Mrs. Crawford shook her head and pulled Tabitha's arms up. "Dahhlin', one can't rest now. There are plenty of folks waitin' to meet you." Tabitha groaned and followed her mother to a group of women wearing gowns. "Ladies, this is our daugtah, Tabitha. We're leavin' for Galstanberry tomorrow." They all nodded in approval.

A woman twirling a bundle of pearl necklaces around her fingers spoke up, "To be a Galstanberry girl is a great honor. I was fortunate to wea that beret and blay-zah in 1975."

Mrs. Crawford laughed, "Gertrude, I didn't know you were an alumnus."

Gertrude! Ugh! What a horrible name!

A short woman with a blonde bob touched Tabitha's dress. "My, oh my, this dress is absolutely stunnin'.

Chiffon?"

"Organza." Mrs. Crawford corrected.

"I see…" The woman responded with her eyebrows raised.

Samuel approached the group and tapped Mrs. Crawford's shoulder. "Excuse me, ladies, my speech is comin' up!" She turned to Tabitha, "Make sure to mingle," then waved goodbye to the ladies.

Getrude patted Tabitha's arm reassuringly. "Don't worry hun, we'll turn you loose." While walking away, she overheard one of the women whisper, "Doesn't look a thing like Sandy or William!" Another spoke in lower tones, "And that red hair! Whea does it come from?" Instead of turning around, Tabitha rushed to the nearest restroom. She pushed the door open, dipped her hands under the faucet, and splashed her face.

Stupid hair!

Suddenly, the restroom door slammed open. "I can't find her! And I've looked everywhea!" The person went into the first stall and locked it. "Jayne, I'm tryin' my darn-dest it!" Tabitha tiptoed near the stall and knocked.

"Hold on Jayne. Someone's in here, so go away!"

"Come out and make me!"

Savannah swung the door open. "Tabs!! We've been

lookin' all over for you! Well, Jayne's at home, but she's been checkin' in."

Tabitha walked over to the mirror. "Is it that bad?" Savannah closed her phone, "Is what bad?" Tabitha lifted a strand of her hair.

"Who cares? It's fabulous and so are you!" Both paused and then at the same time shouted, "I'm sorry!"

Tabitha put her hand on Savannah's shoulder. "With a better diet and more exercise, you can be skinny like me in no time. And don't worry; I don't blame you and Jayne for being jealous of my fab life." Savannah looked away uncomfortably while Tabitha peered at her blush kit.

"Now, which colah will look best?" Savannah pointed to plum. "That's what I was thinkin', too!" The girls hugged, though not genuinely, and left the restroom for separate tables.

• • •

Governor Crawford approached the microphone, "I'd like to thank everyone for comin' tonight! It's your support that's goin' to help me serve Texas again!" Applause filled the hall. "During my tenure as Gove-nah, our great state has lead the nation in reducin' emissions and advancin' renewable energy sources." He held his hand to halt the applause, "And thanks to my ability to build on the strategies of my predecessahs, everyone breathes cleaner air. That's right! Take a whiff!" The crowd laughed. "Smells good, don't it? Howevah, my job is far from ovah. Tabitha, please stand up."

Wha—What?!

"Doesn't she look lovely tonight? My daughtah has been fortunate to be accepted into the Galstanberry Girls Academy. Few girls in the country receive this opportunity. And that ain't how it should be!" The ballroom roared with cheers of agreement. "My educational reform guarantees that Texans get the best education right hea in their own backyards!" Everyone jumped to their feet and clapped enthusiastically. Tabitha looked around the room.

I'm soo goin' to miss my fab life!

When the fundraiser concluded, Governor Crawford stayed behind while his wife and daughter left in a limousine. Tabitha rested her head on the window. "Tonight was fun."

Mrs. Crawford removed a glass of Perrier from the ice box. "It always is! You dost protest too much!"

Tabitha laughed, "Queen Gertrude in Hamlet! When I was little, you read it to me almost every night." Her mother took a sip, "It was your favorite."

"No, my fave is *Romeo and Juliet*."

"Oh, Tabitha, I'm in no mood to debate." She closed her eyes, while Tabitha stared at the night sky.

• • •

In her bedroom, Tabitha applied a cucumber mask, crawled on the bed and stared at the chandelier.

I'm actually leavin' tomorrow!

"Miss Crawford, have you finished packing?" Tabitha sat up and began counting on her fingers. "I've got outfits for free Fridays, ridin' clothes, and mini-versions of my purse and shoe collections." Sophia frowned, "And, how 'bout pencils, notebooks, and bindahs."

Tabitha laid back down. "Yes, duh!"

"Good. Please remove yah mask soon." As she walked out of the room, Tabitha called out, "Take care of Sandy and William, alright?" Sophia nodded and closed the door.

Tabitha washed her face and sat once again at the vanity bench. While chewing a chocolate covered raisin from her candy bowl, she opened her diary and wrote:

Galstanberry, a new castle for a fab princess.

Beverly Hills, Michigan

August 7, 2010

Dear Diary,

Last Wednesday, I received my acceptance letter from Galstanberry. I skipped out on telling you sooner because I'm not exactly 'jumping for joy.' And, of course, Dad, a.k.a. the newest member of the FBI, opened the letter FOR me. Isn't reading other people's mail illegal or something?!

Ugh! He tries to control everything— friends, clothes, and NOW my mail! Let me explain: I, like most kids, never get REAL mail. Email and text don't count! So, when a letter comes, it's like WHAT?! As usual, Dad utterly ruins it for me. It wasn't always like this...

If I go to Galstanberry, and that's a BIG if, I'd let my team down.

Decisions, decisions! To be or not to be a Galstanberry Girl, that IS the question!

Sincerely,
NISHA

Nisha

Sunday, August 29, 2010

"Just call me Alvin, Simon, or Theodore—my cheeks are certifiably, unquestionably, indisputably huuuge! And my new haircut, gosh, WHAT-WAS-I-THINKING!!! Obviously Seventeen Mag's 'must have styles' aren't always accurate.

The mirror reflected a pretty, yet sad, face. Her eyes drifted to a gold picture frame that contained a Polaroid of her family smiling ear-to-ear and wearing Mickey Mouse ears. The Disney trip and Betseyville luggage were gifts for her tenth birthday. Feeling nostalgic, she pressed the frame to her chest and clicked the heels of her favorite caramel ballet flats. If it worked for Dorothy, maybe it could whisk her family back to their *Brady Bunch* times.

What happened to us?

She immediately shook the memories out and slammed the frame face down on the dresser.

"Forget about it! What's done is done!" Suddenly, her phone beeped. "Great! What NOW?!"

> **Dictionary.com:** Word of the Day-
> Evanescence- (v.) to disappear gradually;
> vanish; fade away

"Ugh! Even my cell feels bad for me!" As she slowly closed the phone, her eyes returned to the picture. "If disappearing were only that easy…"

"Nisha! Niiishaaaa!" Dr. Mohan yelled with urgency in his voice. She jumped up from her seat in front of the vanity mirror and began searching each desk drawer for her yellow flashcards. "Yes, Dad, I'm almost ready! Just looking for something!"

Where are they?! Think, Nisha, Think!

She retraced her steps from the bedroom door. "Okay, after dinner I walked upstairs to finish my Shakespeare paper on the computer. Then, I answered Phil's thousandth call about wearing an Oxford blou—" She rushed to the closet and found the cards between her purple Steve Maddens and zebra-striped Kate Spade flats. "Gotcha!" She then pulled an H&M blazer from the hanger and fumbled with the buttons. It was a little snug, but still fit. In the full length mirror, she turned from side to side. "Im-peccable!"

"Niiisha Mohaaan, you're going to be late!" Her father stood at the bottom of the stairs tapping his watch. "Fifteen minutes! Fifteen minutes for breakfast young lady!"

"I'm not hungry!" She protested while dragging her flats into the kitchen.

Dr. Mohan poured Cheerios into a bowl. "It's good for you. The brain—"

"Stop! You're an engineer, not a neurosurgeon!" As he reached for regular milk, she opened the skim milk carton instead. "Skim milk means slim me. Get with it, Dad!"

"Nisha, why do you worry about such things? You are perfectly fine."

"Puh-lease, you have to say that. It's like in the father handbook or something."

The two ate in silence. She avoided his curious stares, while he faked (but, not well) reading the newspaper. After ten minutes, Nisha poked the paper with a spoon. "I'm ready."

"Where is your bag?"

While her flats slapped the wooden stairs, he called out, "And don't forget your notebook and pens!"

Silence accompanied the car ride like an annoying guest. At one time, their conversations were effortless. Now, it was like moving a boulder up an oil-slicked hill. "Nisha, there's a twenty in the front compartment of my briefcase." She rolled her eyes as she pulled his bag from the backseat.

"Twenty's exorbitant, don't you think?"

"Well, it will cover pizza and dessert for your team's victory." A smile crept on her lips. "You ARE the only reason they win these competitions." He nudged her shoulder.

Gosh, is leaving me alone so hard to do!

While some people flipped a coin, or went with their gut, Nisha used lists to make decisions. She removed a notebook from her pink Coach purse and begun to write.

Pros

(1) He'll leave me alone

(2) I can talk 2 someone again

(3) I'll get a new purse

(4) I'll smile, even if for a few minutes…

Cons

(1) He'll expect me to talk about my "feelings" Yuck!!!

(2) I can't be mad anymore

(3) I have too many purses!

Hmm, four to three. Guess its time to talk.

"Thanks for the money. And you're right; the team would be nothing without me!" She paused and looked down at her hands. "Sometimes, I wonder what mo—Oh, nevermind." Her head turned to look at the trees whizzing by. The car slowly drove toward a group of kids standing outside University of Michigan's Law School.

"Nisha, I know it's been difficult, but—"

"Daad!! Yiiield!!"

A tall girl with her ponytail swishing back and forth, ran towards the car as it screeched to a halt. "Nish, I've been waiting for you!"

She turned to her father, but he spoke instead, "Good luck, and…"

"And what, Dad? I don't have an eternity!"

"And good luck, that is all." He turned uncomfortably and looked at the steering wheel. Her heart yearned to say, "I understand." Instead, she half-smiled, shut the door, and weakly waved goodbye.

Tiffany rushed to put her arms around Nisha's shoulders. "First, luvve, your new Coach daahling." Her BFF's obsession with East Coast accents always lightened her frequent somber moods.

"Tiff, your elaborate imitations aren't going to automatically transform you into an East Coaster." They walked into the auditorium and sat in the red cushy seats.

"Sheesh, Nish! English, please! Do you like read the

dictionary for fun? Wait! DO NOT answer that!" She fluffed out her bangs and leaned in like a top secret was being revealed. "Okay, I've got the 4-1-1 on the other teams."

Nisha popped a wintergreen tic tac into her mouth. "Proceed. Oh, want one?"

"No thanks, got a peppermint." She stuck her tongue out as evidence. "Sooo, Crescent has a perfect record like us. Their secret weapon is Brian Alexander, basically a guy version of you."

Nisha rolled her eyes. "Tiff, must we go over this at every competition."

"Well I—"

"Look, Crescent, like every team here, is just made up of amateurs—plain and simple."

• • •

When every seat in the auditorium was filled, a short woman carrying a manila folder approached a wooden podium. "Good morning and welcome to University of Michigan's Debate Tournament. My name is Linda Silverman and I serve as the tournament chair. I am also a Constitutional Law professor here at Michigan."

"Her tweed Chanel is gooorgeous." Tiffany whispered to Nisha, who readily nodded in agreement. Phillip, their third team member, rolled his eyes. "Please, spare us the fashion forecast."

Mrs. Silverman motioned for adults wearing red name cards to join her. "These professors represent different departments at Michigan and will be your judges today. Each school has two teams that will compete in three rounds. Now, for the scoring rules." She put on a pair of glasses and opened the folder. "Each individual will be scored from twenty-two, the lowest, to thirty, the maximum. Teams must achieve scores above eighty in each round to qualify for the championship, which will be held in this auditorium. Third through eighth place will be given to teams earning the highest scores. Teams' scores will be posted during the hour lunch break." She closed the folder and smiled at the crowd. "Teachers, room assignments are located on the second page of the welcome booklet. Good luck everyone and see you in the afternoon!"

Mr. Siegel looked up from his folder. "Okay, I need you to listen carefully and write this information down. Team One, Matthew, Rick, and Alyssa; you're in room 345 for rounds one through three. And Team Two, Nisha, Tiffany, Philip; you're in room 125 for rounds one through three. Got it?" They nodded. "Remember, don't get knocked off your game. We've practiced hard to get this far." Nisha signaled for all of them to lean in. "And don't forget the Four S's: Signal, State, Support, and Summarize."

"Exactly! At noon, I and the other coaches will be in

the cafeteria, which is on the ground level. Good luck!"

Each member put their hands in the center and shouted while raising them, "Gooooo Bronson!" Team One boarded the elevator for the third floor, while Team Two headed towards a door with a chart taped to it.

• • •

Tiffany traced her finger along the paper and pointed to the boxes with their initials.

Round	Proposition	Opposition	Judge
1	Bronson, NTP	Sequoia, AGI	L. Alder
2	Brown, WGT	Bronson, NTP	M. Jones
	Break		
3	Bronson, NTP	Williams, RAS	A. Smith

"Alright, N.T.P., we have two props and one op."

Philip rubbed his hands together and smiled confidently. "Should be a breeze."

Two podiums, with two chairs beside them, were positioned at opposite sides of the room. "Hello, teams. My name is Lorenzo Alder and I am one of the three judges for rounds one through three. To my left is Ms. Mary Jones." Her gold bangles clicked as she waved. "And, to my right is Anthony Smith." He nodded and held a pen in the air. "Each of us will be moderating a portion of the debate. We want you to leave any and all nervousness at the door."

"Easy for him!" Philip whispered to Nisha.

"As judges, our job is to not only score your performance, but also provide valuable critiques that can be used for future competitions. Now, without further ado, let's begin! Up first is Bronson on the side of proposition and Sequoia on opposition. Can the first speakers of teams Bronson and Sequoia approach the podium? Team members, please sit beside the podium in speaker order. Remember, first and second speakers have five minutes, while rebuttals are three. The topic for Round One is, 'Peer pressure is more beneficial than harmful.'"

Philip wrote some notes, rubbed his chin and then began, "There are two sides to every coin. Movies like *Mean Girls* give peer pressure a bad reputation. Today, I would like to challenge that stereotype. Peer pressure CAN be positive. For example, let's say George, a shy and not so confident sixth grader, is getting C's in math class. But, his classmates are achieving A's and B's. George will look around and wonder, 'Why can't I ace stuff too?' He's been positively pressured to study harder and become academically astute.

Throughout this debate, my team will provide evidence that peer pressure IS beneficial. And furthermore, it can be a powerful tool that encourages kids to succeed."

The judges bowed their heads to write. Afterwards, Mr. Adler called out, "Proposition speaker, please begin."

A tall boy wearing a black suit cleared his throat. "Peer pressure is defined in the kid community as 'everyone else is doing it'. Although positive peer pressure does happen, as mentioned by the opposing team, it doesn't happen as frequently as negative pressure. If we use the George example, then we have to look at the WHOLE picture. He may push himself too hard to get good grades." When the tall boy paused to dramatically rub his forehead, Nisha rolled her eyes.

Give-me-a-break!

He continued, "Today, my team will provide compelling evidence to prove that peer pressure is NOT beneficial because it encourages kids to develop bad habits in order to fit in."

Judge Jones checked her watch and announced, "Second Proposition Speaker, please begin."

Tiffany approached the podium, wrote a few notes and began. "We often look at the negative side of things. But, hey, it's what sells right? Movies show violent scenes and the news rarely gives us good things to talk about. Who wants to hear about a fire fighter that helped a girl's kitten? Or, a high school team that raised money to fund a trip to Washington? Positive peer pressure happens more than we think. My opponent is correct; kids sometimes skip school because 'everyone's doing it.' But that VERY reason can teach them right from wrong. Should I skip because my friend's doing it? Or, not skip because it's wrong and my parents would disapprove?

In conclusion, peer pressure is essential to adolescent development because it teaches kids right from wrong."

Judge Smith nodded to the next student at the podium. A girl with curly red hair cleared her throat. "My team would like to advance to our closing. We feel enough evidence has been provided."

"What?!" Tiffany remarked quietly.

Judge Smith turned to Nisha's team. "Do you approve?" They nodded. "Sequoia, your team's request has been granted. We will move to final rebuttals. Please begin."

The girl launched her attack, "Today, we have demonstrated that peer pressure on the whole is negative. Again, the George example is not completely accurate. Infact, it's dangerous to label George's situation as solely positive. 'Why you ask?' Because it's destructive and can lead to low self-esteem.

Peer pressure is often used to bully, and as our opponents admitted, even encourage students to get involved in inappropriate activities. Our team is not advocating for negative pressure. We wish students weren't afraid to stand up to their friends. But, in reality, the 'everyone else is doing it' reason wins." The girl smiled confidently at her teammates as she sat down.

"Thank you. Final rebuttal, please begin."

Nisha approached the podium. "Positive peer pressure is important, and maybe even more than negative. Our opponents keep stating that positive peer pressure just doesn't happen as much as negative peer pressure. Even if that's true, it doesn't lessen its impact on kids.

Peer pressure is positive because it helps kids make important decisions and thus build critical thinking skills. Whether the right or wrong choice is made, at least they are thinking of all the options.

In summary, peer pressure is an opportunity for kids to critically think about their world. And, frankly, there's nothing negative about that."

She sat down and twiddled her thumbs. "Nice job, Nish!" Tiffany whispered as she patted her arm.

At the end of round three, Mr. Alder walked to the front. "Thank you, teams, for your hard work. Now, please collect your belongings before proceeding to lunch. Scores will be posted on this door around 12:30." As the three entered the cafeteria, Philip's eyes immediately spotted the dessert section. "Yes, ice cream!" When he left, Tiffany blocked Nisha's path.

"Tiff! What are you do—"

"Don't look! I think that's Brian Alexander at the table to your right."

"What? How do you know?"

"I facebooked him."

"Excuse me?! You're stalking people now?!"

Tiffany leaned against a wooden column. "I've never seen a bow tie look so a-dorable!"

"Bow tie? Sounds like a certified geek to me."

"Nuh uh, he's like Brad Pitt in a bow tie." Before she continued, Nisha pulled her to the pizza line. "But, But!"

A man wearing a tall chef hat stopped buttering garlic bread as the girls approached. "Good afternoon, ladies. What can I get ya today?"

Nisha's tapped her chin. "Hmm, I'll take a veggie slice."

"Chips?"

"Definitely!"

Tiffany squeezed her shoulder. "Tsk, tsk, Nisha! Cal-o-ries!

"Right, I forgot." But in truth, she was way too hungry to remember. "Fruit cup instead, please."

Tiffany pointed to another veggie slice. "I'll have this one, just without the green peppers. And, a fruit cup, too." Suddenly, a dark-haired boy with deep green eyes stood next to Nisha. "Sir, I forgot to ask for chips."

Tiffany softly shrieked, "Thaaat's him!" He peered at Nisha out of the sides of his eyes. She huffed annoyingly, "Didn't your parents teach you not to stare?"

His eyebrows rose in astonishment. "Well, I…"

"I'm Nisha and unlike you, I was NOT raised by wolves!" Before his mouth opened for a response, a plate of chips with a pickle was thrust in his face. "Here ya go."

"I didn't ask for a—"

"Look, kid, are we gonna have a problem?" He shook his head and then quickly turned to Nisha, "Enjoy your lunch, IF you can."

She rolled her eyes and then walked with Tiffany to their team' table. "How did it go?" Mr. Siegel asked as he cut his spaghetti. Nisha placed her tray down and smiled. "I don't want to be too confident, but…"

"Championship, here we come!" Tiffany finished as they high-fived.

"Score's up! Scores up!" A boy yelled excitedly. Tables shook as kids rushed to their competition rooms. This time, when Tiffany traced her fingers along the chart, she couldn't stop them from trembling.

"Okay, okay, Round One, our score is eighty; Round Two, um, eighty again; and Round Three, a score of eighty-five!!!" Philip slammed his notebook on the ground. "That's 245! We qualify!!!!"

• • •

The cafeteria, which was bustling with excitement only a few minutes ago, had transformed into a quiet and anxious environment. Students at some tables passed around tissues, while others strategized their next move.

"Wait!" Nisha shouted as she blocked the paths of Phillip and Tiffany. "C'mon Nisha, I only have ten minutes to get more ice cre—!"

"No, I'm serious! Do you see that?" She pointed to their team's table.

"Yeah, whose dog died?" He joked.

"Exactly! We can't scream and yell when we say our scores. Got it?" Her teammates solemnly nodded. They walked to the table wearing super serious expressions.

"I knew I did a terrible job!" Sarah remarked as she buried her nose into a tissue.

Matthew shook his head. "No, I used corny jokes during my arguments."

Mr. Seigel's eyes desperately searched Nisha's expression for any signs of hope. "Please say you have good news!" Tiffany leaned into the table and whispered, "We're in!"

"Yessss!!" The team shouted.

"Shh, Shh! Calm down!" Mr. Siegel motioned for everyone to sit and lean into the table. "Now, the hard part. Who's going to represent the team for the championship round?"

"Nisha. She's the best," Tiffany answered quickly. Matthew nodded in agreement. "I concur. But, let's vote; hands in the air for Nisha." Everyone's arms immediately shot up.

"Are you ready?" Mr. Siegel asked. She looked at him sternly and answered, "Always!"

Philip turned to look at the other tables, "So, what other team qualified?" They all glanced around the cafeteria.

"It's probably Crescent," Matthew guessed as he dipped a fry into ketchup.

Tiffany snatched her purse off the table and grabbed Nisha. "We'll go find out!"

The Crescent team was deep into conversation until the pair approached. "Hey, my name's Tiffany and this is—"

"Nisha, right?" Brian Alexander answered with a smirk on his face. "Yep. We're just checking around to see what team made it to the championship." Brian Alexander stood up. "We'll be there, you?"

Nisha and Tiffany exchanged smiles and remarked in unison, "Amateurs."

• • •

The dimly lit auditorium had two podiums on

opposite ends. A pitcher of water and six glasses sat on a table positioned in the center of the stage. Once again, Mrs. Silverman approached the microphone. "Good afternoon, and welcome to the Championship Round! The six judges sitting at the center table will score this round. From left to right: Mr. Lorenzo Alder, Ms. Claire Jackson, Mr. Andrew Smith, Ms. Mackenzie White, Dr. Philip Brooks and Dr. Ellen Rosenberg. The team with the highest score will be our champion. Are we ready to begin?"

"Yeeeeah!!!"

"Can the representatives from Bronson and Crescent join me on stage? Crescent will represent proposition at the right podium, and Bronson will represent opposition at the left podium. The topic is: <u>The music industry should censor music videos.</u> You two have three minutes to compile your arguments." As Nisha and Brian Alexander wrote notes, the clocked ticked away. "Okay, your three minutes are up! Proposition speaker, please begin."

Brian Alexander fixed his bow tie and began, "The music industry influences millions of kids around the world. But with this power, comes great responsibility. Censoring ensures that artists are accountable for their lyrics and music video content.

Some argue that the violence and nudity seen in videos reflects reality. But, that's not true. Showing these images glamorizes this lifestyle; telling kids it's only cool to have a Mercedes or make lots of money, even if it's done illegally.

And what's the big deal anyway! We rate movies by labeling them PG-13 or R. Why not translate the same accountability to artists' videos?"

The judges wrote their scores and then signaled to Nisha. She approached the podium and looked down at her notes.

You can totally do this!

"The first amendment of the United States Constitution grants Americans the freedom of speech. Censoring music videos violates the right of artists to express themselves. Music videos are an art form used to communicate ideas and emotions. They don't glamorize, but comment on reality. Art imitates life, isn't that the famous phrase? Whether it's Norman Rockwell depicting Americana in his paintings, or Jay Z rapping about the harsh life on the streets of Brooklyn; each person's experience is different.

"Music is also a way to escape our reality and experience someone else's. School is definitely not easy for me to deal with all the time. Some days are great and…" She paused and thought about the picture from her Disney trip. "And other days, I feel like hiding under the covers until I'm eighty!" The auditorium laughed. "But, music videos helps us cope with those days. To censor music, is to limit this comfort blanket and our rights as American citizens."

Nisha carefully sat down and rapped her fingers against the edge of the seat.

After 10 minutes, Mrs. Silverman patted on the microphone, "Attention! Attention, everyone!" The auditorium gradually grew quiet. "We are ready to announce the scores. Brian Alexander received a score of twenty-nine and Nisha Mohan a score of thirty. The winner of University of Michigan's Debate with a composite score of 275 is Bronson Preparatory Academy!" The auditorium erupted in cheers. "Can the entire Bronson team and coach join me?" The students ran down the aisles and jumped on the stage. "I would like to present this check for five-hundred dollars to Bronson's coach, Mr. Siegel, and the trophy to Miss Nisha Mohan!

"The UofM debate committee would like to thank everyone for competing today and wish all of you a prosperous school year!" She then covered the microphone and turned to Mr. Siegel. "Make sure your team doesn't leave. There are local reporters that would like to interview them and take pictures."

After the press left, Mr. Siegel gathered both students and parents in the parking lot. "Before we all disperse, I want to thank everyone for a terrific debate year. It has truly been an honor to coach this team. I want to especially thank Nisha Mohan for stepping up to the plate today and helping us to win our first championship!" Everyone applauded.

While Dr. Mohan and Nisha walked to their car, Tiffany ran behind them. "Nish! Nish! Some people are celebrating at Café Venti. Want to come?"

Nisha faked a look of concern. "Sorry, I have to pack."

Dr. Mohan smiled. "We are ordering pasta tonight. You are welcome to join us."

Nisha glared and nudged her father. "Tiff, really I can't—" But it was too late; she had left to ask for permission.

In a matter of seconds, Tiffany returned breathless. "My mom says it's okay."

In the car, Nisha smiled at Tiffany, but frowned at her father in the rearview mirror.

"Nish, are you ready for a calor-bration?"

"A what?"

"It's calorie and celebration fused. Clever, right?" Tiffany smiled proudly while scrolling through the menu on her phone. "Okay, pesto herb bread. Sound good?"

"Sure."

"And what toppings does your little heart desire?"

Nisha laughed, "Remember Tiff, I'm vegetarian."

"No prob, meat goes straight to the hips anyway."

The car pulled into the driveway of a red brick bungalow. "Tiff, the phone's by the fridge. You order, I'll be right back."

• • •

Nisha closed her bedroom door quietly and began tiding the room. She placed shirts in the dresser and returned purses to their rack. After a few minutes, there was a knock at her door.

"Nish? Can I come in?"

"Wait a sec!"

She rushed to place the gold picture frame in her desk drawer. "Okay, enter!"

"Your dad just left to get the food."

"Good! I'm starved." Tiffany nodded and sat on one of the suitcases. "Are you sad to be leaving?" Nisha shrugged. "Yes and no. I'll miss our gossip sessions." They both smiled. "But, a change of scenery will be good for me." Tiffany jumped on the bed. "Well, like the great Diana Ross song, *I'll survive.*"

Suddenly, Nisha's phone beeped.

> **248-232-1512:** Is this Nisha?
> **NISHA:** Who r u?
> **248-232-1512:** Brian Alexander from
> comp 2day

"Nish, what's wrong? You look like you've seen a ghost or something!"

"A random number pops up on my phone."

"Yeeah?"

"And the person says its Brian Alexander…"

Tiffany instantly looked away. "Really? That's kinda weird…"

Nisha moved closer to her. "Is it? Or did you give him my cell?" Tiffany walked over to the purse rack. "Did I ever tell you how fab your bag collection is?" Nisha sighed. "Well, what do I say?" Tiffany raced back to the bed. "I thought you'd never ask. Give me the phone!" Before Nisha could protest, Tiffany's fingers were texting a mile a minute.

> **248-232-1512:** Gr8 job 2day
> **NISHA:** U 2 :)
> **248-232-1512:** Can't believe ur talking

> **NISHA:** ?
>
> **248-232-1512:** I was raised by wolves,
> right
>
> **NISHA:** O, LOL!

Nisha desperately grabbed at the phone. "Give-it-to-me!" Tiffany fervently shook her head. "Trust me!"

"Trust you? You stalk people, and then give my cell number away. Ex-cuuuse ME for having doubts!" Tiffany ran down the stairs with the phone held to her chest. "Nishaaa! It's good for yoooooou!!!"

Nisha followed her into the kitchen and stood with her arms folded. "Good for me? What does THAT mean?"

Tiffany looked at the floor. "Well, you know…"

When Nisha stepped closer, Tiffany stepped backwards. "Fine, I'm not going to chase you. But, clarify PRONTO!"

Tiffany looked at her suspiciously. "Promise?"

Nisha pulled out a chair and sat.

"Well, you've changed. After what happened, you don't smile or laugh as much."

Nisha rolled her eyes. "Don't be dramatic. Plus, if I'm sooo awful, why do we still hang out?" Tiffany also sat. "Because you're my B.F.F, like a sister, even." Nisha bit her lip and squeezed her hands together. "Sooo many things are different. And I just don't know how…" Tiffany ran to hug her. "It's okay, Nish, really. Whenever you want to talk about it." Nisha gently pushed her away and walked to the refrigerator. "I don't. So, want some O.J.?" Tiffany nodded and slowly returned to her seat. It was normal for Nisha to shut down when conversations turned personal.

"Nisha?" Dr. Mohan called as he struggled through the front door.

"Yeah, Dad?"

"Can you and Tiffany help me with the food?"

They rushed to the front door and carried the boxes to the kitchen. "Ooo, this pesto bread looks delicious!!"

Nisha nodded while picking cheese from her fingers. Dr. Mohan looked over a pizza box, and asked, "Tiffany, are you excited about school?"

She took a sip of Coke. "Totally, Dr. Mohan! New teachers, different classrooms, cuter boys! I mean cuter, um, nicer buildings! Anyway, I'm definitely going to miss Nish. She's like my partner in crime."

Dr. Mohan raised an eyebrow. "Partner in crime?"

"Dad, purely a figure of speech."

"Of course, Nisha, I wasn't born yesterday." The three laughed and continued to eat.

• • •

After an hour, their stomachs were about to explode.

\<Ding Dong, Ding Dong\>

When Dr. Mohan left to answer the door, Tiffany whispered, "Don't forget you-know-who."

"What?"

Tiffany peeked around the corner. "Brian Alexander, re-mem-ber."

Nisha grabbed the phone and flipped it open.

248-232-1512: ??
248-232-1512: ??
248-232-1512: Got 2 go, have fun @ G!
ttyl

"He's gone!" Tiffany stared dreamily at the ceiling. "You two will be like Romeo and Juliet; separated by distance, but united by love."

Mrs. Rockefeller entered the kitchen clapping her hands. "Nisha, your father tells me two congratulations are in order. First, for the Galstanberry acceptance; and second, for pulling the team to victory. My daughter will surely miss your positive influence." Tiffany grabbed her mother's arm and moved to the door. "C'mon, Mom, it's soo time to go." On the porch, father and daughter waved to the departing car.

"Nisha, we have to talk for a minute."

Just ruin my fun, like always.

"Dad, I'm reeeally tired."

"This won't take long." They walked into the kitchen and sat down.

"Last month, I received news that I've been laid off."

"What?!"

"It's only temporary for engineers."

"Can we not afford Galstanberry anymore? How about my designer stuff?" Her father tried to respond, but only worst-case scenarios raced through her mind. "Dad, I can't live like Cinderella pre-ball!" He fixed his glasses and wiggled his nose.

Uh oh, that's not good.

"Nisha, I've saved enough. However, there is still a portion I simply can't afford. And then for the spring semester, I'm just not sure." Nisha looked at the table. "So, what's going to happen?"

"Galstanberry has been very accommodating with our situation."

"Our situation? Ugh, that sounds awful!"

"Nisha, listen to me. You have been granted a partial academic scholarship."

"Scholarship!!" She shrieked. "Only poor kids get those! What will people say?!" Her father shook his head in frustration. "It's an honor to receive an academic scholarship, an achievement! Sometimes I just don't understand you. Maybe if your mo—"

"Stop!" She looked at him sternly. "Don't you say her name, don't you say it!" She ran upstairs and slammed the bedroom door. She paced the room while shaking her head.

Think Nisha Think! No one has to know!

She ran to the purse rack and threw every designer She ran to the purse rack and threw every designer bag she owned into the suitcases. "More shoes! I need more cute shoes!" After sitting in her closet for an hour, it was finally time for bed. She snuggled into her favorite Ralph Lauren P.J.s and opened her diary to write:

To a new life, a new beginning, and maybe,
just maybe, a new me...

Welcome Home!

Monday, August 30, 2010

"Headmistress Tissel, the students have begun to arrive!" She swiveled her chair around and watched limousines to Lamborghinis smarm the campus like bees to honey. "Sarah, I requested mint tea over ten minutes ago. Where is it?" The secretary blushed. "Oh, I'm so sorry, Headmistress! With all the activity on campus, I just—"

"The more you talk, the longer I wait."

She scurried out the door.

Headmistress Tissel continued to gaze onto the busy campus. She smiled at the pink "Welcome Home!" banner that waved from Campus Square. There, girls excitedly registered for Orientation. Parents stood close by to ensure that names, long and short, foreign and common, were spelled precisely right. Royal purple balloons waved in the wind from the residence halls and class buildings they were tied to. The crescendos of Beethoven's fifth symphony emanated from Carillion Bell Tower.

A taxi slowed down as it approached the perfectly manicured grounds. Inside, Mr. Garcia nudged Lillian and whispered, "¡Estamos aquí[1]!" Her eyes widened as the cast-iron gates drew near. Across where the two gates met was a shield with a large curly "G" in the center.

I'm livin' hea?

As she continued to look out the window, a blonde girl dressed in a velvet violet blazer emerged from the stables riding a strawberry roan horse. "Papí, I didn't know they had horses!"

"Yes, for your ridin' lessons!"

Ridin' lessons?

• • •

At Campus Square, a pair of stylish cowboy boots stepped out of a shiny black limousine. "Sandy, I don't know why she brought her entiah room." Governor Crawford shook his head while two butlers struggled with his daughter's suitcases. Tabitha rolled her eyes and opened an Evian bottle.

"Fa-thah, promise that you won't embarrass me today." Mrs. Crawford fixed the brim of her straw hat and sighed. "That's his job, dahhlin', to embarrass us." They laughed and approached the registration table.

[1] We are here

"Welcome to Galstanberry! What is your name?" Tabitha pulled her Dior sunglasses down her nose, "Tabitha Crawford," and then positioned them back up. The woman flipped through sheets of paper, and then crossed out her name. "Here is your Welcome Packet and room keys to Albright Residence Hall. Inside is a map of the campus and schedule of activities. Have fun!" Tabitha threw the items in her Longchamp tote, stuck her nose in the air, and briskly walked toward her father. "Dahhlin', slow down! I need to see the schedule. Your fa-thah needs to tell the butlahs whea to put your bags!"

My bags…Good point!

Tabitha slowed her pace and handed the folder with her orientation papers to her mother. "Let's see, we've already registered and ate breakfast…" Mrs. Crawford looked up and shrieked excitedly, "Now, we can see yah fabulous room!" Tabitha admired her new French manicure.

Room, shmoom.

"Tabitha Kay Crawford! Are you even listenin' to meh? Look at this schedule!" Tabitha reluctantly bent the paper towards her.

Welcome to Galstanberry!

Orientation Registration   8AM-4PM
Campus Square

*Tours of class buildings and athletic facilities are available
8AM-3PM

Continental Breakfast   7AM-10AM
Ivy Crescent

Residence Hall Check In   10AM-4PM

Afternoon Tea   12Noon-2PM
Pomeroy Hall

Note: Berry Boutique & Books is open 9AM-2PM only.
Books can also be purchased online.

After examining the map, Governor Crawford's pudgy finger pointed east. "That-a-way!"

• • •

Inside Albright Residence Hall, Brandi, her family and the other girls waited in the royal blue living room. Its stone fireplace, hardwood floor, and mahogany armories made it appear as though it was plucked straight from the early 1900s. "This place is like an antique store! Seriously, everything looks expensive and really old!" Brandi remarked as she admired the room's furnishings. Tamara nodded, "Yea, Sis, and you're living in it! So, if you break it, you buy it!"

"Attention, everyone! Attention!" The room gradually settled down. "Welcome to Albright. My name is Stacey Selman and I am the resident HouseSister." People quietly chuckled as Tabitha and her parents snuck in the back. "Yes, you heard right, HouseSister." Her auburn curls bounced up and down as she nodded. "We are referred to as 'sisters' because we consider your daughters as members of the Galstanberry family. My job is to ensure that Albright runs smoothly, which means enforcing the rules and making sure your daughters feel comfortable. Each floor has a living room and kitchen; complete with stove, refrigerator, and microwave. Does anyone have an idea why this residence hall is named Albright?"

A short girl wearing a red sundress raised her hand. "Yes, the girl in crimson."

"Is it named after Madeline Albright, the first woman Secretary of State?"

Stacey smiled and folded her arms. "Have you been reading my notes?" The group laughed as the girl nervously spoke up, "I-I did a book report on her for Women's Month. She is kind of like a mentor to Hillary

Clinton, the Secretary of State now."

"Show off," Tabitha mumbled as she flicked her Juicy jeweled butterfly charm.

"Impressive, and you are?"

"Tracey Sandstone." The girl blushed while her parents smiled proudly.

"Impressive, Tracey. To embrace the accomplishments of women in the nineteenth and twentieth century, each Galstanberry residence hall was creatively renamed after women who were the first in fields like science, politics, medicine; you get my drift. Now, a little about moi. I am twenty-three and a graduate of Mount Holyoke, a women's college in Massachusetts. I received my Bachelors in Art History and Français. After graduation, I lived in Paris and studied art works at the Musée du Louvre for a Masters program at NYU." She interlocked her fingers under her chin, and then looked at the ceiling. "My dream, dream, drrrream job is to be a curator at the MET in New Yawk." Everyone laughed. "I am also the tutor for French courses 101 and 202. Are there any questions?" Governor Crawford raised his hand. "Yes, the gentleman in the back!"

"How about security?"

"Good question. Residence Halls can only be accessed by student ID cards." She held hers in the air. "We also have our own police force that patrols twenty-four hours. If there are no more questions…" The group looked around. "Then, you are excused to check out the rooms. Please remember that Afternoon Tea begins promptly at noon." Brandi removed one key from a small envelope and smiled, "Room 321."

As the Johnson family boarded the elevator, Tabitha's parents enjoyed coffee in the living room. "Are you guys finished yet?" Mrs. Crawford stirred her cup and motioned for her to sit. "Dahhlin' your room is not goin' any-wheah. We'll see it in a minute." Tabitha stomped her foot. "You said that ten minutes ago!" Governor Crawford brushed the cookie crumbs off his lap as he stood up. "Sandy, our daughtah is correct. We havta maintain a schedule." Finally, they squeezed into the elevator with another family. As Tabitha reached for an elevator button, a little boy pressed each one. She sarcastically huffed, "Thanks a lot!" And then gave an unsympathetic look to the apologetic mother and embarrassed sister.

• • •

In Ivy Crescent, Fei and her family enjoyed Continental breakfast at a tall coffee table. Their feet humorously dangled from its tall chairs. "That bagel tree is definitely cool! How do you think it stays up?" Dr. Chin sipped a glass of apple juice and responded with immense pride. "Science, a miracle of science."

Here we go again...

Mrs. Chin pointed to Carillion Bell Tower through the window. "And Fei, very smart engineers made that."

"Sorry-I-asked." She remarked quietly while finishing her blueberry muffin and flipping through the Welcome packet. After a few minutes, she perked up. "Okay, my room's next!" Dr. Chin shook his head, "The schedule says you can tour class buildings. Your mother and I would like to see the science classrooms and laboratories."

"C'mon, Dad! You work in a lab, seeing another one can't be THAT exciting!" Her parent's facial expressions remained unchanged. She jumped off the chair and sighed, "Fine, fine, let's go check it out." The family walked westward towards a tall brick building with a greenhouse attached to the side.

• • •

On the northern end of campus, Lillian looked at the map, then up at a large, arched stone door. "I guess this is it." She and her parents followed the flow of girls inside. A woman with an "Ask Me" tag directed people to a circular room. Tucked in the corner was an ivory Petite

Grand piano, and lining the room's perimeter were Italian-style olive fabric couches with walnut wood trim.

"Everyone, please file in," requested a tall girl as she leafed through a binder. When the room was filled to her satisfaction, she closed it and looked up. Her perfectly round bob framed her face and highlighted her green eyes. "My name is Pavlina Gobach and I am the HouseSister of Morrison Residence Hall. I graduated MIT in 2009 with a Bachelors of Science in Physics and Chemical Engineering." The parents nodded, obviously impressed. "Many of you are probably wondering why an aspiring physicist is at a junior high boarding school." She paused and let out a small chuckle. "That's exactly what my parents asked, too!" The group laughed.

"But, I wanted a change of pace. And I think this is the perfect place to do it. One day, I'll be an astronaut or discover another atomic particle. But right now, I am your daughter's HouseSister and the math and science tutor, of all levels, for Morrison. By the way, can anyone guess the importance of this residence's name?" Mrs. Garcia nudged Lillian, who immediately whispered, "No sé."

"Yes, you do, Lilly!"

Pavlina eyes searched the groups' faces. "Does anyone know the answer? Don't be shy!" The girls looked around to see who would be brave enough to respond first. "Okay, here's a hint." She dramatically placed a hand over her heart. "At some point in life the world's beauty becomes enough. You don't need to photograph, paint, or even remember it. It is enough." Mrs. Garcia's arm shot up. "Great! We have a parent participant!"

"My Lilly knows the answer." Everyone turned around as Lillian stepped back and shook her head fervently. "Lo si— I mean, I don't know."

"She does!"

"Mamá, no, I do not!"

Mr. Garcia nervously cleared his throat. "Anyone else?" Pavlina gave a sympathetic smile and directed the attention back to the front. "No worries, Lilly. That is your name, right?" She nodded, but looked to the floor. "Our residence hall is named after Toni Morrison, one of my favorite novelists and the first African-American woman to win the Nobel Prize for Literature." She reopened her binder. "Alright, I need a single file line right here." While Lillian squeezed between two girls, Nisha and her father wandered into the building's lobby.

"Excuse me, where is residence check in?" Dr. Mohan asked the woman with the "Ask Me" tag. "Through there, sir." Nisha jumped in line as her father looked through the Galstanberry brochure.

The girl in front of Lillian smirked, "I can't believe your mother did that!"

"Yea, she loves to tawk."

"Tawk?"

"Yea, tawk, what's wrong?"

"Nothing, I just thought people only TALKED like that in movies." Before Lillian could respond, Pavlina tapped her arm. "Deep in thought, huh?" She shrugged. "You are room 424, and here are your keys."

As Lillian walked back to her parents, she shook the girl's comment out of her mind.

Today is my day, and no one's gonna ruin it!

Her father picked up her suitcases, "Where are we going?"

"Cuarto piso[2]!"

The three rode the elevator and then walked down a long hallway. "Here it is, my door! MY DOOR!" She stared at it, as if in a trance, until her mother cleared her throat, "¡Si! Now open YOUR door, before YOUR mother and YOUR fat—"

"Yea, yea!" Lillian turned the lock and pushed the door open. Her black ballet flats gently stepped on the shiny wood floor.

"Lilly, these bags aren't light, ya know."

"Oh, sorry, Papí, put them next to the bed by the window." She walked around the room and touched each piece of furniture.

[2] Fourth floor

When her father opened the closet, she gasped and ran inside it. "It's huge!! Jalissa and Camilla would be soo jealous of me right now!" Mrs. Garcia sat at the desk. "Lilly, we have to tawk."

What did I do this time?

"You knew the answer to that question, didn't you?"

Lillian pondered for a minute, and then slowly walked out of the closet, "Yea, I just didn't feel like answerin'."

"Como no[3]!"

"Because someone else probably knew the answer. I was givin' them an opportunity."

Mrs. Garcia looked at her husband and sighed. "Lilly, you received the scholarship because you worked hard and weren't afraid to answer OR ask questions." Mr. Garcia placed a hand on his daughter's shoulder. "You're smart just like the girls hea. Don't be afraid to show it." Lillian nodded and then smiled, "I think makin' my room cute will help me out. Can we get started pleeeeease?" Her parents nodded and tried to suppress their smiles.

• • •

Back in Morrison's living room, Pavlina busily searched a pile of envelopes.

[3] Why not?

"I know your keys are here!"

She then peered at the long line.

"Okay, there are other girls that need keys too. If you and your dad can give me about 20 minutes, I can go to the office and see what's going on." Nisha plopped down on one of the couches and pouted.

"Great, I'm a nomad on my first day of school!" Dr. Mohan patted her hand. "Don't worry, the issue will be resolved shortly. I will not leave this campus until you have a room." One by one, each girl received her keys and proudly showed them to her parents.

Ugh! That-should-be-me!

As time passed, the room gradually emptied. "Dr. Mohan, Afternoon Tea begins at 2p.m. When you return, I will have your daughter's key and she can settle into her room." Nisha rolled her eyes. "So, what should I do with my bags? Just drag them around like some homeless person?"

"No, you may leave them here. I will make sure to store them in a safe area."

"Here, with you? I DON'T think so!"

"Nisha!"

"Dad, she's already lost my keys! She's obviously not responsible enough to watch my bags!" He turned to Pavlina, "Please excuse her, she is nervous. The bags will be left with you."

• • •

When noon approached, girls and their parents made their way to Pomeroy, a pale yellow building with a dome shaped top. As Fei and her parents climbed the stairs, Brandi and her family followed close behind. "Bàba the lab tour took for-ever! I didn't even see my room!" They approached a cream linen table with two girls seated behind it.

"Hey, welcome to Afternoon Tea! What's your n—"

"Fei, and these," She looked to her right and sighed, "Are my parents, Dr. and Mrs. Chin." A girl with hazel eyes and a curly ponytail searched the table then handed over four items. "Here are your name tags and table number." Fei reluctantly lifted her suitcases. "My parents wanted to see the labs so—."

"You haven't seen your room," finished the second girl, as she blew her long bangs out of her eyes. She reached across the table and grabbed the suitcases. "Don't worry, we'll just hide them under this table. I'm Sarah Rizzo and she's Donna Williams. We're 7th, well now 8th graders here. Just look for us after tea." As Fei's parents walked away from the table, Fei leaned in and whispered, "I can't WAIT for freedom." She then ran behind her parents into the ballroom.

They sat at a round table covered with a Gamboge table cloth and decorated by quaint cherry tea cups and paisley napkins folded like fans. The Waterford crystal vases, which overflowed with Hermosa roses and orchids, sparkled from the center of the table, like a star in the midnight sky.

Meanwhile, Brandi and her family arrived at the second check-in booth. "Brandi Johnson with 5 guests." A girl with long braids smiled and distributed 5 name tags and one table number. "Thanks!" While Mr. Johnson took the boys to the restroom, the rest of the family navigated through the crowd to find their seats. When Brandi sat down, a girl with two long pig tails whipped around and gripped her arm, "You've saved me!"

"Saved you? From what?" Fei discreetly pointed to her parents, who happily chatted with Dr. Johnson. Brandi laughed, "No prob! I'm Brandi, but you can call me Dee. This is my sister Tam."

"Hey, nice to meet ya!"

"And, I'm sure you can guess my mom. Jamal and Michael, my twin bros, and dad will be here in a sec."

"It must be cool to have a big family."

"Sometimes, but they drive me ka-razy though!"

Fei looked at her parents again, "Believe me, I know exactly what you mean!"

• • •

A tall woman sporting a purple tweed jacket and matching skirt gracefully ascended the stairs of a raised platform and spoke into the microphone.

"Hello everyone and welcome to Afternoon Tea. My name is Dean Simmons and I am the Dean of Etiquette and Decorum." She touched her bun to ensure it was as proper as her posture. "Tea time is a fine tradition here at Galstanberry. Please raise your hand if you have participated in a tea before." Tabitha excitedly lifted her arm, and whispered to her mother, "I hope they have Rose Petal tea." Lillian quietly tapped her fork against her water glass.

"Hey! What's Rose Petal tea like?" Tabitha sighed and rolled her eyes in response.

"Look at all of those hands! Do not worry if you are a tea newbie. Today, everyone will learn and have fun together!" Applause echoed throughout the ballroom.

"The first course will be freshly baked raisin and apple scones. You may spread the Devonshire Clotted Cream or Strawberry Preserve with the small knife to your right." Waiters wearing white gloves, orange vests and matching bow ties, placed baskets filled to the brim with scones on the tables. "This totally makes up for my key fiasco." Nisha remarked through chews. A girl seated next to her gushed, "Don't they just look absolutely gooorgeous!"

"You sound just like my friend Tiff. She'd love these!" The girl stopped eating mid bite and placed her scone on the plate. "Do you think you'll get homesick? I mean, we ARE moving away from, like, EVERY-BODY."

"Probably sometimes, but look at this place! It's beauteous!"

"Huh?"

Nisha let out an exasperated sigh. "Beauteous, you know, beautiful, grand? My mo— Nevermind."

The girl shrugged and continued to eat.

Waiters returned with steaming fuchsia tea pots engraved with golden berries.

"Our famous Galstanberry Tea is made and served on this campus only."

Lillian lifted her spoon and shook the liquid in the round bowl part. "It's light purple!" Mrs. Garcia looked at her husband in surprise. "This is your first tea, right?" Tabitha asked as she scooped sugar cubes into her cup. Lillian nodded. "Then let me warn you, it's really biddah!" She pushed over the sugar bowl. "I ALWAYS need these." Mrs. Crawford shook her head. "That's 'cause you have a sweet tooth daahlin.'" When Tabitha sipped, her eyes widened and cheeks turned bright red.

"This stuff's très sweet!" Lillian smirked and pushed the sugar bowl back. "I guess you AREN'T the tea expert then!"

• • •

At table 10, Nisha constantly flipped her phone open.

Ugh! When is this going to end!

"Nisha, your luggage is going to be fine!" She sipped her tea, but was too worried to relish the taste. "Coach, Juicy, Dior, those are all great bags she could sell to—."

"Enough!" Dr. Mohan sternly whispered as a waiter placed an assortment of mini triangular shaped smoked salmon, chicken and cucumber sandwiches on the table. Nisha rolled her eyes and sipped once more. As she surveyed the sandwich platter, she noticed that her neighbor had already piled six onto her plate. Nisha nudged her and whispered, "Slow down! It all goes straight to your hips anyway."

"Really?"

"Trust me!" She winked.

• • •

When the short hand on the Grandfather Clock When the short hand on the Grandfather Clock moved to two, Dean Simmons rung a bell to prompt the waiters to clear the tables. "Thank you all for participating in Afternoon Tea! I, along with the Galstanberry faculty, would like to wish the parents, very safe travels home.

And to our new Galstanberry Girls, we look forward to officially inducting you into The Galstanberry Girls Academy by our traditional Pearling Ceremony tomorrow morning!"

At that moment, it dawned on every girl that this Galstanberry world was now theirs. Each eye widened and lips smiled as they pondered their new reality.

. . .

As parents drove out of the campus, each light post blinked then dimmed, casting a faint yellow haze. Girls returned to their residence halls overflowing with curiosity, apprehension, and most of all, enthusiasm for the journey that lies ahead.

The Girlz of Galstanberry